Witch's Valley

BEVERLY L. ANDERSON

PHOENIX VOICES ANTHOLOGIES

Copyright © 2024 by Beverly L. Anderson

All rights reserved.

No part of this publication may be reproduced, distributed, or transmitted in any form or by any means, including photocopying, recording, or other electronic or mechanical methods, without the prior written permission of the publisher, except as permitted by U.S. copyright law. For permission requests, contact Phoenix Voices Publishing, 7901 4th St. N, St. Petersburg, FL, 33702, 727-222-0090.

The story, all names, characters, and incidents portrayed in this production are fictitious. No identification with actual persons (living or deceased), places, buildings, and products is intended or should be inferred.

Beverly L. Anderson asserts the moral right to be identified as the author of this work.

Beverly L. Anderson has no responsibility for the persistence or accuracy of URLs for external or third-party Internet Websites referred to in this publication and does not guarantee that any content on such Websites is, or will remain, accurate or appropriate.

Designations used by companies to distinguish their products are often claimed as trademarks. All brand names and product names used in this book and on its cover are trade names, service marks, trademarks, and registered trademarks of their respective owners. The publishers and the book are not associated with any product or vendor mentioned in this book. None of the companies referenced within the book have endorsed the book.

Dedication	1
Introduction	2
1. Chapter One	3
2. Chapter Two	12
3. Chapter Three	23
4. Chapter Four	34
5. Chapter Five	45
6. Chapter Six	54
7. Chapter Seven	65
8. Chapter Eight	75
9. Chapter Nine	85
10. Chapter Ten	96
Epilogue	105
About the Author	110

Also by Beverly L. Anderson 113

To Megan, my newest Bestie. You've made me smile more times than I can count. You're an amazing friend. I'm happy to write in this series.

Introduction

Welcome to a retelling of Hansel and Gretel! I know, that's not really a fairy tale that goes into retelling very often, is it? It was an intriguing challenge to write up a story based on that fairy tale, and I am really happy with the way it turned out. Of course, there are warnings associated with this as it is a dark fairy tale. Hansel and Gretel (Drew and Scarlett) are much older than their fairy tale counterparts, and there is love in the air as well. Mind the triggers, please.

Trigger Warnings

Non-Consensual Sex/Rape
Captivity/Kidnapping
Blood and Gore
Explicit Sex
Non Consensual mind altering substances
Death

Chapter One

The Woodcutter's Dilemma

Charles Chambers had a problem, and his wife believed she had the perfect solution. He was reluctant to do what she wanted him to do, but he also knew he had to do something. Winter was coming, and as they lived a good two-day journey on horseback to Sapphire City, they could not just go there for help. Not that Charles would ever step foot inside that place again, in any case. He had chosen to live in the woods on a small parcel of land he managed to buy with his meager earnings as a factory worker before his children were born.

Charles had a problem in that he could not feed his family through the winter. He had a wife and a pair of twin children, a boy and a girl. His wife, Gracelyn, believed they should take the twins deep into the forest and leave them to fend for themselves near Witch's Valley. She, of course, had little connection to the twins, as she was their stepmother. Their mother had died during childbirth, and Charles had married Gracelyn right afterward so she could help take care of the babies. She never made a connection to them, though, and did not consider them her children.

"Do you wish to starve this winter?" she demanded as they sat in the kitchen of their log cabin, one that Charles had built.

The room was warm from the stove and the nearby hearth that was roaring with a strong fire. A too bright rug decorated the floor in front of the heath, something that Gracelyn had brought with her when she married him. The wooden framed sofa had threadbare and flattened cushions on it, but it still served its purpose to them as giving them a place before the fire. The small dining table had just enough room for the four people in the household, and though Charles had built the furniture many years ago, it still was sturdy. It was dinged, banged up, and chipped in places, and one of the chairs had broken several years ago, but Charles always fixed things that broke. He was especially good with wood and carving intricate figures. Gracelyn chastised him for it, though, telling him that it was a useless hobby.

"You cannot feed four people on what is in the storehouse. The two of us will be lucky to make it through the winter as it is. Which do you prefer? We can all die together, or you can send them on their own to survive if they can."

Gracelyn had brought up the fact that their stores were depleting fast this year. Charles had no idea why. He had saved the same amounts of grains, cured meats, and dried fruits as every year before. Somehow, they were running out, and while he thought it strange, he had no idea why Gracelyn would lie about the storehouse. He supposed he could have gone to check the stores himself, but he trusted her. He had no reason not to.

"We could take them to Sapphire City," he suggested. As much as he never wanted to step foot in the place, he was able to consider sending them alone.

She scoffed at the thought. "And do what with them? Leave them there instead of the woods? They are more likely to fend for themselves in the valley. It is rich in winter berries, snow hares, and everything they need to survive. They can take the valley north if they want, and climb out the other side, and return to Sapphire City. You don't seem to be understanding, this, Charles. Here, they will die. Out there, they may survive, as will we. They are grown. It is time for them to be on their own."

Charles didn't want to send his children off to the valley, no matter how old they were. He wanted them with him, as they were all that remained of his dearest wife. She had been the light of his life, and though he could never tell Gracelyn this fact, he missed her fiercely. Gracelyn had never, could never, take her place in his heart. He felt tears rise to his eyes and shook his head.

"I can't."

"You coward," Gracelyn shouted, her light blue eyes hard in the dim light of the evening. "You will cause us all to die. At least in the valley, they have a chance."

He stood and left, hearing her snort in annoyance. He walked outside and saw his son, Drew, chopping wood for the fire. He had not even asked him to do it; he had just noticed the wood pile was shrinking. Drew was not great at chopping wood, as he had little muscle for it. He tried his best and split the smaller logs that he could manage. His sister, Scarlett, sat on the steps and watched. Both of them shared so many features. They had the same red, nearly orange hair, full of loose curls. Their eyes differed slightly, as Scarlett had brown in her eyes, making them hazel, while her brother's eyes were deep green. He smiled because they looked just like their mother. How could he even consider sending them to their fate alone in the valley?

A few days passed, and Charles once again sat in the dining room with Gracelyn. For dinner, they had little to eat as they were trying to use up the last of the stores that might go bad during the winter. The twins never complained; instead, they ate their meager portions and thanked them before they went to do their chores.

"You need to reconsider, Charles." Gracelyn would not let up on the issue. "Something must be done soon. The stores will deplete quickly once the first frost happens. You need to make sure we survive to make it through the winter!"

Charles sipped the weak tea that she had made, and thought it tasted strange. He wasn't sure what it was in the tea that made it wrong, but there was something there. He shook it away and felt something strange come over him. It was an overwhelming desire to do as Gracelyn asked. He set his eyes on her and blinked a few times. His head was growing fuzzy, and even though he didn't know why, he wanted to please her more than anything in the world. He wanted to make her happy, even if it meant sending his own children away to fend for themselves.

"I will do it," he said after a few moments. "They are nineteen. They know how to survive, and I want to give them a chance. I will take them to the river so we might fish tomorrow, and then I will leave them there."

Scarlett overheard her father as she stood outside the doorway. She put a hand to her mouth and rushed to tell her brother.

"Drew!" she urgently whispered as she came outside, where he was struggling to split larger logs than the day before. "Father is going to leave us at the river! What should we do?" she asked.

Drew frowned. "I don't know the way back from the river, nor do you. I know, gather as many white stones as you can. We'll leave ourselves a trail we can follow back to the house."

That afternoon Drew and Scarlett were sitting on the steps when their father came out. "We're going to the river to do some fishing, so gather your supplies, and come along," he said, not even looking at them.

Scarlett looked at Drew and stood up, and they slowly got the fishing poles and everything they needed. As they walked, Drew dropped the white rocks along the path. For some reason, it felt like they were taking a very long time to get to the river, as though they were winding their way through the wood. They were going through areas that Drew had never seen before. Finally, they reached the river, and their father sat down the supplies he'd brought and got situated with the poles.

The river was not very big, perhaps ten feet across, and for the most part, the area they had come to was calm. There were a few small rapids in a couple places along the river, and they could see fish swimming in it. It was a good fishing spot, and one that the twins had been to before. Of course, when they had come before, their trip had not taken nearly as long, so Drew had the idea that they had meandered through the wood so that the twins would be confused and unable to find their way back.

Drew was worried about what his sister had overheard. He glanced back and saw the last rock he'd dropped. They had a path back, though, so they would be able to make it should their father actually leave them at the river. After an hour or so, their father stood up and looked at them.

"I forgot something at the cabin. I'll return in a moment," he said, and not waiting for any sort of response, left.

Drew watched him go, in some sort of horror, realizing that what Scarlett thought she'd heard was true. He was leaving them in the woods. He looked at his sister after he had gone, meeting her eyes.

"What should we do?" he asked.

"We go home," she said, putting down the pole and standing. "We left a trail, and we shouldn't let that woman push us out of our own home with our father."

Drew nodded and put his own pole down. "Wait, let's put these somewhere safe. Just in case we need to come back for them."

Scarlett reluctantly agreed, putting the poles and supplies in the brush beside the river. They carefully picked their way along the path they left, which they felt was longer than it should be, and this time Drew was sure that this path was not the way they had always come before. They got to the cabin well after dark and knew that it probably hadn't taken their father that long to get back. He would have taken the direct route, the one that the twins could not remember since it had been years since they'd been taken to that point on the river. They marched up to the door and found it locked from the inside. That, in itself, was strange. But they ignored it, and Drew knocked on the door. Around them, the smell of rain was increasing in strength, and they both knew that a storm was coming. They feared in more than one way.

A moment passed, and the door opened, showing their father. He stared at them without speaking for a long time. A look of confusion settled across his scrunched brows, as if he didn't know what to say to them.

"Father, let us in! You left us at the river, but we found the way home!" Scarlett said, her face twisted into a furious mask at this. "Why would you abandon us? Why would you leave your own children to fend for themselves in the woods? What happened to our father?"

"Who are you?" he asked. "I don't know you."

Drew felt his heart sink and stomach turn. "Father, what do you mean?"

Their father stared at them for another few moments and shook his head.

"Gracelyn?" he said, turning to look in the house. "Do you know these two strangers?"

Their stepmother came to the door beside their father and smirked at them. "Why, no, my dear. I don't know them. My dears, are you lost in the woods?"

Drew was stunned into silence, but Scarlett spoke up. "What do you mean? You've raised us since we were babies! I heard you tell him to leave us in the forest to fend for ourselves! What have you done to our father?"

"I'm sorry, I don't have any children. My wife, Gracelyn, is barren."

"Yes, but you had us with our mother, before you married her!" Drew finally had found his voice. "Remember, she died during birth, leaving you a widow. You married Gracelyn to help take care of us!"

Their father looked at him with curiosity for a moment. "I think you are mistaken. I've never known anyone to love besides Gracelyn here. I've had no other wives, and I certainly don't have any children. I think I would remember things such as that. Please, I hope you find who you are looking for, but it is not me."

With that, he closed the door, leaving the twins stunned and silent on the step.

"What has she done?" Drew whispered after a moment.

Just as they started to debate what to do at the door, a peal of thunder resounded around them, and raindrops began falling. They looked around for shelter, but the only place to go was the storehouse.

"Hopefully, they haven't locked it," Drew said as they scrambled toward the stone building.

Scarlett got there first and hauled the heavy door open. They managed to get in before the rain came down in force. It was dark inside, as there were no windows to keep as much weather out of the building as possible. Drew fumbled on the wall for the light switch. He got it, and the room flooded with garish light from a lone, naked bulb in the ceiling.

Scarlett gasped as she looked around the large room full of shelves. "We have plenty stores!"

"She told Father that we were going to run out this winter, but there is a lot here!" Drew agreed as he walked down the shelves and took stock.

The shelves were full of dried fruits, glass jars of vegetables, meat, and other canned goods, as well as wrapped cured meats, and barrels of grain sat at the end of the shelves. Pickled vegetables, stews, and more lined the shelves as well. They were definitely not going to run out of stores this winter. They had stocked like they had any other year.

"I don't understand," Drew muttered, running his hand over the glass jars of pickles. "Why would she say we were low on stores?"

"She wants us gone for some reason." Drew looked around the room unsure what to do.

Scarlett nodded in agreement. "And she's done something to Father to make him believe we're not his children. Something is going on and we've got to figure out what to do about it! We can't just leave and let her do whatever she has planned."

"Yeah, but what gain is there? Father is a poor woodcutter. He never goes to Sapphire City, you know that. He won't even consider letting us go to school or anything because he won't set foot in the place. So, he agreed to train us to take care of ourselves. He doesn't have anything he could possibly want." Drew frowned and crossed his arms.

"Maybe she just wants him." Scarlett leaned against the shelves to stare at Drew. "I mean, think about it. Father loved our mother with everything he had. He never really loved her. And he's still in love with

Mom, even thought she's gone. Why else would she do something to make him forget her and us?"

"She must be a witch," Drew surmised. "Otherwise, how would she accomplish all this?"

"I know, let's find the witch of the valley, and see if she can help us!" Scarlett said.

Drew thought about it. "I don't like the idea. We don't know if she's good or evil. What if she won't even help us?"

Scarlett shook he head. "We have to try. For our father. We can't leave him with Gracelyn thinking he loves her. We can't let him forget our mother."

Drew sat on a barrel and Scarlett sat beside him. They held each other as the storm raged outside, wondering what would become of them.

Chapter Two

To the Valley

The storm let up after a few hours, and Drew and Scarlett wondered if it was a good idea to spend the night in the storehouse. If Gracelyn came out in the morning, they could confront her, and maybe they would know more about what was going on. They opted to wait, to find out what they could.

It was an uncomfortable night, and quite cold. They had managed to find a couple of old, threadbare blankets, and had covered with them as they sat up against the barrels along the back wall of the storehouse. Elusive as it was, they managed to find some sleep. Even thought they knew the confrontation with Gracelyn would come, they still managed to rest some. There was no way to tell time in the storehouse without windows, so when the door opened, they both were startled awake.

"What are you doing here?" came the shrill voice of their stepmother.

Drew and Scarlett stood and came over to the door where she held it open.

"What have you done to our father?" Scarlett demanded.

Gracelyn smirked again, lip curling against her too white teeth. "I want his love."

"For what reason?" Drew said after a moment. "Why can't you be happy with him as he is?"

For a moment, nothing happened, then Gracelyn's face morphed into a horrific visage of some kind of demon. Fanged teeth lined her mouth, her blue eyes changed to glowing red orbs, and she laughed in an inhuman sounding voice. "I will devour him once I have had my fill of his love."

"What are you?" Scarlett said with a gasp.

"Some call me demon, some call me a succubus. My favorite meal is that of old widowers who have been forced to forget their loves. I take that love, and I consume it until there is nothing left, then I devour them entirely. Once I'm done with your father, I will move on to someone else, and there's nothing you can do to stop me, foolish children that you are." Her face morphed back into the familiar blonde-haired and blue-eyed woman that had raised them.

"Why now?" Drew asked, unphased it appeared by her transformation while his sister appeared shaken.

"It is time. I've waited long enough for all signs of his wife's life to disappear, and then when it was apparent that you were not going to leave, I made the decision to force you out. I cannot convince someone of their devotion when there is someone else that has their love. Simple magic, and something you will never break." She smiled again, showing too many teeth when she did so.

"And what if we destroy you?" Drew asked, still standing tall and not flinching from the demon before him.

"Oh, you can try. You will not succeed. Say you did, though, then your father would be free of my ensnarement, and remember everything. However, you will not destroy me," she said, confidence lining her every word. "Now, begone, before I do kill you."

She stepped back so they could leave. "Why don't you kill us? There's nothing stopping you," Drew said as he led his sister through the door, wet grass crunching under his feet.

"You pose no threat to me, and it amuses me to watch humans suffer, especially those who will feel keenly what has been done."

Drew wanted to do something, but he had no weapons, or even any way to fight this kind of threat. "We'll be back. And we will destroy you."

"Like I said, you can certainly try. You will not succeed any more than others that have tried before you," she said, walking into the storehouse and grabbing food for breakfast. She smirked at them as she passed them, returning to the cabin.

"What should we do, brother?" Scarlett whispered. "We can't fight a demon."

"No, but we can find someone who can," Drew said, his voice firm and sure. "We go find this witch and see if she can help us. That's what we need to do."

* * * * *

"What are we to do?" Scarlett said as she sat on a tree stump halfway to the entrance to the Valley.

"We find that witch of the valley, and we get her to tell us how to kill a succubus," Drew said, still not perturbed in the least by the fact their stepmother was a demon.

"How can you remain so calm about this, brother?" she asked, exasperated and exhausted by the walk through the forest.

It was at least five miles from their house to the entrance of the valley, and they had walked it without stopping. Now, finally, as huger began to gnaw at both they stopped to assess the situation. Drew sighed, looking around the bushes for berries. He did not find any around them. He was not pleased with their luck so far at finding food.

"I just want to get our father back, is all," Drew said at length.

Scarlett shook her head, pulling down on the t-shirt she wore and sighing. "I'm glad I didn't wear any of my nice clothes," she muttered.

Drew nodded. Both of them had worn clothes that were old and comfortable, considering they were supposed to be fishing. That was a good thing since anything else would have been ruined and made their lives so much harder on them. Drew swept stickers off his pant legs and came back from looking for berries.

"We should move on," he said. "We still have a ways to go."

"I know," Scarlett said, standing up from the stump. "Maybe we'll find some berries or other late autumn fruits."

Drew knew it wasn't likely. The winter berries were not out yet, and the rest of the fruits from summer were gone already. He supposed that he should have gone back for the fishing equipment, but the storm had washed mud over the path, and the white stones leading to the river were long gone. He had thought of using bread to mark a path as they left, but then he realized the birds would just eat it, so it didn't matter if he left a path back or not.

"When we get to this witch's house, how do we convince her that we need help?" Scarlett asked as they walked on toward the valley.

"We don't give her a choice. If she isn't willing to help us, we make her help us." Drew didn't look back as he spoke, and for once, his voice was strong.

Drew had always been a meek boy. Even growing up, he followed whatever his sister did. He didn't branch out on his own, at least, not when people noticed it. He thought in different ways from her, but in action, he was demure, quiet, and unnoticed. He didn't speak much, and rarely, if ever, argued with anyone over anything. He accepted what others said, and generally did as he was told. Of course, it wasn't like he ever saw anyone except his sister and his parents. Out where they lived, there were no visitors. Even their school had been done through the mail.

Scarlett walked behind him, and he led her toward the valley.

* * * * * *

Gracelyn smiled as she set dinner on the table. The spells had worked perfectly, as they always did. Charles had no memory of his previous wife, and he had no knowledge of his children. She hummed a little tune as she spun around the kitchen, the yellow apron floating in front of her. She came out, bringing the drinks to the table. She sat her drink down and placed one beside Charles. She leaned over him and kissed his cheek, then inhaled his soul's essence.

A succubus could survive infinitely off the life force of humans alone. It wasn't necessary to kill them at all. Simply siphoning off a bit of life force here and a bit there, they would shorten their lifespan, but in exchange for a few years, a succubus could feed. So far, after 19 years with Charles, he had lost at least ten years of his life to her. Of course, he would lose the rest now that she was in the last phase of her consumption. She had prepared her morsel carefully, and with more care, it would be delectable. She would enjoy consuming his soul in its entirety.

"My dear, will you allow me to provide for you?" she asked. "I know you are ill the last few days, and too weak to cut wood. You have plenty of wood stored, however, so please rest instead."

Charles nodded. "Yeah, there's enough for a few months," he said.

Gracelyn sat down at the table and ate the meal slowly. As a demon, she had no taste for human food, though she could eat it in a pantomime of human existence. She smiled brightly as Charles ate slowly. His health was degrading the more she fed from him. He was past the point of no return, now. It was only a matter of time before he succumbed to her entirely. The sweetest morsel was the one given freely.

* * * * *

Drew and Scarlett made it through to the entrance of the valley as night was starting to fall. The trees took on an ominous presence as they lorded over their heads and made various shadows on the ground. There was a constant breeze, bringing the smell of water toward them from the river where it wound into the valley from the direction they came. While they were close, they had not yet gotten to the river where it merged into the valley.

"What should we do, Drew?" Scarlett asked as they looked around the lush and dark valley around them.

"We can either stop here or press on until we're too tired to go on anymore," Drew said, turning his gaze back to her. "If we press on, we might find this witch's house, and perhaps get a warm bed for the night."

Scarlett shook her head. "What are the chances of that?"

"Depends on how cooperative this witch is with us." He sighed a little and kicked a stone on the path. "I hate that we've been forced to do something like this. We should be home with Father."

"Don't let it get to you, Drew. We couldn't have done anything more than we did. She's a succubus, after all." Scarlett put a hand on his shoulder with a wan smile.

"But what if she was lying?" Drew asked, looking at her sharply. "What if she isn't really a succubus and everything she said was a lie?"

"You saw Father. He had no recognition in his eyes when he saw us. No matter what she is, she's done something to him. I believe her. She's definitely some sort of demon. What benefit would lying have for her, anyway?" Scarlett rubbed Drew's back in slow circles, something she'd done since they were young children to calm any upset in Drew's mind.

"I mean, maybe she just wanted us gone. Maybe there's some other reason Father forgot us. Maybe—"

"Drew, you're being ridiculous. We only have one choice, and that's to find this witch and see if she'll help us," she said, sighing deeply.

Drew nodded, turning away from her and looking further into the valley. In the dark, what should have been a peaceful and serene setting had turned into something nefarious and frightening. The branches screeched where they rubbed each other, the rustling of the leaves indicated something hiding there, and the howling of the wind might seem a wolf in the dark. Drew for the first time since he left his father's house was unsure of what he'd chosen to do. He never made rash decisions, and going off after a witch was pretty rash, now that he thought of it.

"I mean, we don't have any idea what this witch is like. What if she's worse than the succubus?" Drew finally said.

Scarlett shook her head. "How is she going to be worse than a soul-sucking demon?"

Drew had no answer to that. Though, in the distance he saw what he thought was a puff of smoke in the dim evening light.

"Wait, something is up ahead," he said, pointing in the direction he saw the slight bit of smoke.

"I don't see anything," Scarlett said, frowning at him.

"I know I saw smoke, like from a chimney. We should at least go to that point and see what it is," he said, turning toward her with both brows raised in query.

Scarlett nodded, and they headed toward where Drew had seen the smoke. They walked for almost an hour, and were about to give up, but they soon saw they were in front of a small white house. There was a white chimney that gave out a puff of smoke now and then, and they could tell by just being near the house it was warm inside.

"Should we knock?" Scarlett asked.

Drew nodded, stepping in front of his sister, and knocked upon the door. After a few moments, a man answered that took Drew's breath away.

He had rich, wavy black hair that fell to his shoulders and smoldering brown eyes. He was taller than Drew by several inches, perhaps six or more. He was wearing a pair of shorts and an A-shirt that let Drew see all the defined muscles of his chest and stomach. His face was covered in a short bit of stubble, making him look rugged and manly. It made Drew's mouth dry immediately, mostly because other than his father, he'd never seen another man. He was a bit confused by the reaction, though, as he'd never really thought about whether he liked men or women. It was now quite obvious what his preference was.

"Yeah?" the heavenly man said, staring at them with unblinking eyes.

"Um, we're traveling through the valley, and... Well, we don't have supplies or anything, and were, uh, kinda hoping that you might have room to put us up on the floor of your house or something." Drew was positively shaking, he was so nervous about talking to this beautiful specimen of manhood.

The man before him smirked. "Yeah, I got space. It's a one room cabin, though, so one of ya will have to sleep on the couch, but the other can bunk with me."

Drew's protective instincts for his sister overrode any semblance of interest at that moment. He would not let his sister share a bed with some strange man.

"Scarlett, do you might taking the couch?" he asked, not looking away from this man as they stood in the living room of the house.

It was indeed a one room cabin. There was a couch and chair in the front before a roaring fireplace, and on the other side of the room was a large bed. To the side was what looked like a small kitchen area with a table with two chairs around it. The décor was plain, mostly woodsy looking stuff, like a bearskin rug, a mounted deer head on the wall, different things of that nature.

"Are you a hunter?" Drew asked as he looked around.

"Been known to hunt now and again," the man answered. "I'm Borane, by the way."

Drew turned back to see he had extended a hand toward him. He swallowed and shook his hand, feeling his face heat from the blush spreading across it. His grip was very firm and his hands, surprisingly smooth. Drew's hand lingered a bit too long, but he pulled it away after a moment.

"Drew. And this is my twin sister, Scarlett," Drew answered.

"Ah, nice to meet you both. Tell me, what brings you to Witch's Valley?" he asked.

Drew froze for a moment. How much should he tell this stranger. He certainly couldn't tell him about the demon. He'd think they were crazy. Things like demons didn't exist in their world, after all.

"Uh, we need the Witch's help with something. A family affair, you know. That's really all I can say," Drew said and crossed his arms over his chest, still glancing about the room.

Borane looked at him for a moment. "Well, you know, you can hang with me for the night, or a couple days if you want before you move on. I'm out here on my own, and I rarely get company."

Drew looked up him, his green eyes meeting Borane's brown ones, and he nearly lost his breath. He jumped when Scarlett placed a hand on his back. He turned, a little wide eyed and stared at her.

"I think me and Drew would be glad to keep you company, but not a very long time. We do need to get on our way to meet with the witch. Do you know anything about her?" Scarlett smiled and then dropped a subtle wink at him.

"Why don't you come sit down in the living area, I'll tell you what I know and get you some tea," Borane said, gesturing to the couch and chair in the living area.

Scarlett and Drew went and sat beside each other on the couch while Borane went into the kitchen area and began making some tea on the small stove in there. Drew kept glancing at him, noting everything about him. The way they shorts clung to him, a bit tight in the thighs, powerful thighs, and the way the shirt molded against him, and the thick biceps.

"He's nice looking," Scarlett whispered to him.

Dry as his mouth was, he tore his eyes away and swallowed hard. "Um, yeah, I guess so."

"Don't deny it. You think he's hot." She had a slight smile on her lips and Drew stared at his hands.

"Uh, maybe."

A few minutes later, he returned with a cup of tea for each of them, and one for himself. "I hope you don't mind, I sweetened it a little with some honey."

"Oh that's wonderful!" Scarlett said, taking. "Uh...so about the witch..."

Chapter Three

The Demon Hunter's Tale

"Ah, the witch in the valley," Borane said, leaning back and sipping the tea. "That's a story. Goes back to when I was a teenager, actually." He looked over at them. "Are you in the mood for a long story?"

Drew nodded, hypnotized by Borane's thick, baritone voice. It was soothing, and with the tea in the warm room, it was somewhat surreal in a way. He swallowed and watched as Borane looked thoughtful for a moment.

"So, here we go."

***

Borane was trekking through the valley looking for someone, anyone to help him avenge his family. He was sixteen years old, and ready to destroy the brigands that had set upon them, killing his mother and father immediately, and wounding his brother to the point he died days later. He had been able to hid and came out relatively unscathed. He would forever be guilty because of that.

He'd heard of Witch's Valley when he was a child, and his father had warned him never to go near the place. It was said to be full of traps set by the witch to ensnare the unwary. His father had said it would be his death if he went there. Of course, now, he had been forced to make this move because more than anything, he wanted to punish the brigands.

He found a house, and he stood before it. It was a plain log cabin. Beside it was a large herb garden, and there were large berry bushes around the outside like shrubs. He could see fruit trees toward the back of the house. The house itself was log and the door was painted purple. He approached and knocked on the door.

An old, decrepit looking woman answered the door. She had gray hair pulled up in a bun, and a wizened face with a long, thin pointed nose. Her lips were barely visible and pale. She stooped, making her seems even shorter than she was, and she looked at him with eyes that were sharp as a youth's. Their steel gray color was not faded with age, and they pierced through a person to their soul.

"I'm Borane. I need your help."

She chuckled, a sound that was strange in that it almost had an ethereal quality to it. She shook her head. "I don't just help anyone that comes to my door," she said after a moment. "Give me a good reason, then we may trade."

"Trade?" he asked, brown crinkling.

"Of course, you don't think I would offer my services for no return? I may help you, should I decide you're worthy of my help, but you will have to give something to me in return."

"I have no money," he said, shaking his head.

She grinned, stepping back and motioning him into the house.

"I don't trade in money."

Borane walked in, coming into a room that gave him chills. The walls were lined with unusual things on shelves. There were hanging bundles of herbs and flowers around the room held up by ropes that connected to the bare rafters in the ceiling. There were strange masks on the wall, frightening in their visages. He glanced to the left, and saw a large, open kitchen, where there was a large oven, and a huge cauldron bubbling with a greenish liquid in a fireplace.

She walked past him into the living area, where a ramshackle set of furniture was displayed. It looked like it was going to fall apart at the slightest touch, but she dropped into the chair with a comfortable sigh. She glanced at him.

"Well, boy, come, sit." She gestured to the matching sofa. "It doesn't look like much, but it's comfortable."

Borane swallowed and sat down, finding the witch was right. It was surprisingly comfortable. She eyed him. "So, tell me first why you want my assistance."

"My family was murdered by brigands," he said, staring at her.

"Revenge is your motive," she said, nodding. "I do respect that in a person. What do you expect by coming to me?"

"I don't know what I want," he said, his honesty not allowing him to make up a tale. "I was told a witch lived deep in the valley, and was warned never to come here. It was all I could think of to do, so here I am. I don't know what to do at all, but I want to do something about the men that murdered the people I cared for."

The witch nodded. "The path you are seeking is one that may lead to destinations you do not desire. Are you willing to walk it, knowing that?"

He nodded. "I don't care what happens to me as long as I destroy the ones who hurt my family."

She smiled, showing jagged, yellow teeth. "Very well. We begin at dusk. Until then, I suggest you conserve your strength. You're going to need it."

She got up and disappeared into a nearby room, leaving Borane on the couch. He didn't know what to do, but she said to rest, so he laid down on the couch and to his surprise, fell quickly into a deep sleep.

"It's time, boy," he heard and came awake with a start.

Borane sat up and blinked, seeing that the room was now lit by dim light emanating from some location he couldn't see. She had a grin on face, and he wasn't sure he liked that. He got up and followed her out the door. It was dusk, and she was leading him to the small wooded area behind her house. As they came into it, he saw a circle of runes inscribed into the ground. There was a table sitting near the circle, with some items sitting on it, but he couldn't discern exactly what they were.

"You need power, and I can give you power. But there is an exchange necessary for that to happen, and you will need to make the choice about what you're prepared to give." She picked up a steel bowl from the table and began tossing some sort of powder into the circle.

Borane shook his head. "I don't understand what I could possibly give other than my life."

She turned, wrinkled brow arched. "What do you think you will give, other than your life?"

He nodded. "If the brigands are punished, I will gladly die."

She chuckled, putting down the silver bowl and picking up a brass one. "Oh, you won't die. That doesn't benefit me or the forces I work with."

"Forces?" Borane asked as she dropped sprigs of some sort of herb on the circle.

"Forces in the dark. There's a reason people do not come here. I see all that happens in the valley, and I know everything that comes into it. I know what crawls in the dark, and I know the darkness in the human heart all too well."

"I don't understand."

She turned to him. "Long ago, I loved a man. He was a good man. But he changed, became darker somehow. And eventually, I realized he was possessed by a demon. One night, he tried to kill me. He did kill our child. I killed him with my bare hands, despite the demonic forces that powered him. Now, I control those forces for my own desires," she said, nodding as she stepped back. "Now, be silent, boy."

She started chanting in a language Borane didn't know and after a moment, smoke began to rise from the center of the circle. The chanting became more frantic, and louder, and then, from within the smoke, a form began to solidify slowly. Borane's eyes widened, because he'd never seen something like that before. The figure solidified, and he was staring at a creature unlike any other. He was a strongly built humanoid, but he had horns and great black bat-like wings. His eyes were glowing red and staring at the witch.

"Witch!" his voice boomed. "Why have you summoned me?"

The witch seemed unperturbed by this monster that had to be close to seven feet tall towering over her bent form. "I call for your aid."

The creature, or he guessed it had to be a demon, stared at her for a long time. Then he spoke in his booming voice, though it was quieter now. "What is it that you desire?"

Borane could hardly believe what he was seeing. This creature was just going to do what she asked of him? He swallowed, impressed by the power this witch held in her gnarled hands.

"This boy wishes to slay those that have murdered his family. I call upon you to grant him your blessing, and in exchange, I will take his life for your service."

Borane frowned. What exactly did that mean? It wasn't like he was going to argue. He was willing to give up his life, but this was unusually spoken.

The demon chuckled. "The usual exchange."

"Of course," she answered.

"Bring him forth," the demon said, finally looking at him.

The witch smirked and turned to him. "If you are serious in your aim of having revenge, come forward."

Borane didn't hesitate, he stepped up beside her. The demon reached a clawed hand out and placed it against his cheek. "Yes, this boy's heart is pure. I will grant this."

He pulled his hand back and nodded. "It is done."

Borane blinked. He didn't feel any different, so what exactly was done? He swallowed, turning toward the smirking witch.

She made a motion with her hand and the demon disappeared into the smoke. After a few moments more, the smoke faded away. She turned and started to walk away.

"Wait, what just happened?" he asked.

"Come, demon hunter. You've much to learn. What you seek is not human, whether you know it or not, and it is only a matter of time before what you seek finds you on its own." She then walked back to the house.

Borane jogged to keep up with her as she moved surprisingly fast. "I don't get it. Demon hunter? What do you mean?"

She got to the door and motioned him inside. "You'll understand your sacrifice all too soon."

He came in behind her and sat down at the small table. It shifted and wobbled but had a square cover over the round table in lace. He looked around, seeing more strange bottles along the shelves, and was almost overwhelmed by the flood of different scents coming from all corners of the area. She sat down across from him and grinned broadly, showing those jagged and yellow teeth as she did.

"You have to pick something in your life to give up. Something important to you, and something that will be deeply missed. You will give up your heart's desire." She looked him over. "And I'll determine what that is."

He blinked. "How will you decide what that is? You don't even know me."

She nodded. "But the cards do." She leaned over to a drawer in the nearby cabinet and drew out a black velvet bag.

She opened the back, and pulled out a thick stack of cards. She handed them to him. "Shuffle."

He shrugged, staring at the backs of the cards as he carefully shuffled the cards together, making sure he shuffled them well. The backs were black with glittering silver symbols on them that he didn't understand. After he felt they were sufficiently shuffled, he handed the stack back to her.

She hummed to herself as she began placing cards on the table in a cross pattern. Three across and four down. She chuckled. "Isn't that interesting."

"What is it?" he said, staring at the myriads of different pictures on the cards.

"Your heart's desire is a wife."

He blinked and stared at the card in the center of the cross. It was a couple wrapped around each other. "Well, yeah, I mean, isn't that what every man wants? To find true love with a woman and make a family?"

She shook her head. "Not in the way you desire it. No, your desire is deeper than most men. You gauge your value to the world on if you can produce a family and provide for a wife in a sufficient manner. Your heart years for that connection, and to not only have a wife, but the children that go along with her." She pointed to the card next to the lovers card. "Family." She pointed to another. "Continuance." Then to the third, "And this, in this position, it is the consequences of not meeting your heart's desire. Despair."

"So, you're saying I'll never have a family?" he asked, starting to understand what all this meant.

"Your heart's desire of marrying a woman and having a family shall never come to be. Think of it as the curse you have on you now that you have gained the title of Demon Hunter."

He blinked and stared at the cards as though they were going to change into something different, but instead he felt a sinking sensation. "I think I understand. What happens if I try to go against this curse?"

"You will not succeed. Most likely, any woman you approach will be repulsed by you, and you will not be able to even attempt to make a family. Adopting children might bypass the curse, but you will not be able to have your own. You will never touch the flesh of a woman." She looked at him very seriously. "I mean that literally. You will not be able to even touch a woman or a female child. This curse will follow you for as long as you live. And as Demon Hunter, that is a very long time."

She moved to pick up the cards, and Borane moved to stop her by grabbing her hand. As his hand came close to her it was as though an electric charge shocked him and he snatched his hand back. He blinked, frowning at his hand. She was right. He couldn't even touch the old witch. She wasn't lying.

"You believed I would tell you false?" she said, chuckling a little as she slipped the cards into the bag and put it away.

"I didn't think that. I just moved before I thought," he muttered, still staring at his hand.

She smirked at him. "This curse will never go away. You gave in exchange for power. Now, you will be able to destroy those that killed your family."

"How does becoming a Demon Hunter give me the ability to get revenge?" he asked. "I only want to punish these human brigands."

She shook he heard. "You are naïve. You smell of demons when you come here, and you believe it is only a mere human that decimated your family."

Borane shook his head. "I don't understand. How do you even know this?"

"I know the smell of someone being pursued by demons," she said. "They're on your trail. You don't think they let you live out of some sort of pity, do you? No, they let you live to watch you suffer. They've followed you to the edge of the valley, and wait there for you now, because they know to enter my valley is to court their death." She smiled. "But you now have the power to defeat them."

"How will I know what to do?" he asked, frowning as he stared at his hand, flexing it into a fist in front of him.

"The knowledge is there already. You merely have to use it."

***

Drew blinked as Borane stood up, taking his cup to his small kitchen area. "Wait, what happened then?" he asked.

Borane was silent until he came back and sat down, staring at them. "A tale for another time. For now, should we rest?"

Scarlett drank down the rest of her tea, as she had apparently been so enraptured by the tale, she hadn't even drank the tea. Drew wanted to know more, but he felt it would be rude to press the issue. "Uh, okay, sleep is good."

"Very well," Borane said, standing and taking their cups.

Drew noticed how careful he was when he took Scarlett's cup, not coming close to touching her when he did so. So, what he was saying was true. Unless, of course, he was a really good actor. He took the cups and set them in his sink, then disappeared into a closet and came back with blankets and a pillow. He handed them to Scarlett.

"Thank you," she said, smiling, and Drew noted again, how careful he was to avoid touching her.

"And you," he said, smiling at Drew, who felt his heart tremble at the sight. "Come on, you need your rest if you're going to see the witch."

He walked toward the large bed and pulled the A-shirt off over his head and Drew felt week in the knees because he had a perfect V shape to his back, with broad shoulders tapering down to his waist, and his shorts were low on his hips, revealing the swell of his ass. He walked toward him as he got into the bed.

"Come on now," Borane said. "Since you're sharing the bed, I won't sleep naked like I usually do."

"Oh, okay," was all Drew could manage as he slipped under the covers on the other side of the bed.

Borane turned off the light beside the bed, dropping the room into darkness and for a while, all he could hear was the soft breathing in the bed next to him. He was stiff and afraid to move because he didn't want to disturb him.

"You've never slept in another person's bed, have you?" Borane said after a while.

"Why do you say that?" he asked, eyes wide in the dark.

"You're so stiff and laying there like you're afraid of touching me. I can touch you, you know," he said.

At the words, Drew felt a funny feeling in the pit of his stomach. If they weren't in bed next to each other, maybe it wouldn't have sounded so alluring, but touching him was all Drew wanted to do. He wanted to run his hands over his hard muscles and feel every one of them move, and to be under that powerful form... He shook away thoughts like that. He was a guy, why was he thinking of being pushed down like that?

"Ah, sorry," he muttered and turned on his side, facing away from him, still wide awake and nervous.

He felt Borane move a little, then things were quiet, all except his pounding heart.

Chapter Four

Meeting the Witch

After a while, Drew fell asleep. He had dreams of what he wanted to do with Borane, which rattled him as he opened his eyes the next morning. He immediately smelled ham cooking, and something else. He blinked and sat up.

"About time you woke up," he heard Borane say from the kitchen.

Scarlett was sitting on the couch with a plate in her lap, eating. "Thought you were going to sleep until noon."

Drew schooled an obvious problem as he sat there, concentrating on willing the annoying morning erection away. He tried to convince himself it was just a natural reaction to waking up, but down deep, he knew it wasn't that at all. After a moment, he got up and walked into the kitchen and Borane smiled that deadly smile and handed him the plate.

"Thank you, you didn't have to do this," he said, stomach already growling. It had been since the day before when they last ate.

"Your sister said you hadn't found anything along the trail, and I thought I'd give you something before you headed out again," Borane said, turning back to the kitchen and picking up a plate of his own.

Drew sat down beside Scarlett and tried not to eat too fast even though he was starving. He smiled at Borane and nodded.

"You're a good cook," he said.

"Thanks, when you live alone out in the middle of nowhere, you learn a few things," he said.

"How do you get supplies out here?" Scarlett asked, looking over at him.

"I travel about twice a year to Sapphire City. I stock up on anything I can't grow myself, and pick up cured meats to last for the season," he said, taking a bite and chewing a bit. "And I'm sure you didn't notice the barn, but I have a truck that I take into town."

"Ah, that makes sense," Scarlett said. "I imagine you don't use it much."

He shook his head. "No, just for the trip to Sapphire City. It's a long one from here, and the roads aren't good, as you've noticed, so I only go when necessary. The dirt roads here are a mess when it rains like yesterday, so I have to plan accordingly. I think I'm the only one with a house here, aside from the witch, of course."

"I guess people avoid the area because of her," Drew said, savoring the last bite of his eggs.

"Yeah, but that's okay. I like my solitude." He smiled. "What about you guys? You haven't told me anything about why you're wanting to find the witch, or where you're from."

Drew stared for a moment at nothing, debating what to say. He was a Demon Hunter, so maybe he'd deal with the succubus. But what if they couldn't trust him? He wasn't sure what to do. He glanced at Scarlett.

"Uh, well, just some issues that we want to talk to the witch about, you k now. A problem with our father. But I think we can handle it," he said after a moment with a definitive nod of his head.

Borane looked at him with his brow crinkled for a moment, then nodded. "Okay, I get it. Well, you should take a few supplies with you, as it's a good day's hike to her place," he said, standing and going to the closet again.

He rummaged around in there for a bit then came back with a knapsack full of stuff. He handed it to Drew as he took the plate from him. Drew opened the pack and saw dried fruit, nuts, and some jerky.

"This is too much!" he said, looking back up at him. "You shouldn't be giving us so much of your stores!"

Borane gave him a sideways smile. "Don't worry, I've got plenty. I always stock up well and have leftover at the end of the season. Just be careful on your trek. Are you sure you don't just want to go to Sapphire City? I'd be willing to take you."

Drew shook his head. "No, thank you, though. We'll just walk down to the witch's house and get her help. You've done enough," he said, standing and shouldering the pack. "We appreciate everything you've done."

Scarlett sat her own plate beside her and stood, nodding. "Um, yeah, I mean, I'd hug you, but I guess that's not possible."

Borane nodded. "A farewell will be fine, Scarlett."

"Okay, we'll be off," Drew said. "I can't thank you enough."

"It's not a problem," Borane said as they walked toward the door. As he opened it, he squeezed Drew's shoulder. "Farewell, my friends."

Drew nearly whimpered at his touch, but he kept it under control and cleared his throat. "Uh, yeah, farewell, Borane."

Drew walked with purpose for a few hundred feet before he began slowing and turned to look back at the cabin growing smaller. Scarlett smirked as he looked back.

"You liked him."

"A little, I guess," he muttered. "But he's cursed, remember? He can't have a family."

Scarlett was quiet for a while as they walked along the dirt road. Then she spoke up. "He can't have a family with a woman. The witch didn't say he couldn't have one with a man."

Drew blinked and stopped. He stared at her for a moment. "What does that mean?"

Scarlett put a hand on her hip and shook her head at him. "It means, he could have a family with you if you liked each other, dufus."

Drew started walking. "His heart's desire was a woman. He's not going to be satisfied with a man. He won't be happy like that," he muttered.

They walked in silence until the sun was high in the sky. They found a fallen log off the path and sat down, sharing some of the dried fruit and jerky.

"You know," Scarlett said, chewing on a bit of jerky. "I didn't find him all that attractive."

Drew blinked, staring at her. "What? How could you not? Those amazing brown eyes? His silky black hair? Those muscles! I mean, he looked like he worked really hard to stay looking like that. And he has such a nice, soothing voice. I could have listened to his story all night!" He stopped and realized Scarlett was smirking at him. "What?"

"Just you. You really liked him, not just a little. First time you've ever felt that way, huh?" she said. "I mean, it's not like we meet people. It would make sense if guys were your thing that you'd be completely enamored with him. I mean, as far as guys go, he's okay, but I don't think guys are my thing."

Drew paused, dried apple halfway to his mouth. "Wait, what?" he said, lowering his hand. "You mean you think you like girls?"

She shrugged. "Maybe. I'd have to be around some to decide, you know. Or maybe I don't like anyone. I just know, I wasn't too interested in him, even if he had been able to touch women. He obviously was not my thing."

Drew nodded, eating the apple slice while he thought about it. Being sequestered from the world like they were, not even having radios to get music, they just grew up not knowing how they felt about other people. They knew about other people, of course. They had home schooled, and all. So, they knew about cities and towns, and how people gathered and did thing, they just had never been exposed to anyone other than their parents. Really, it was impossible to know what their predilections were until they were face to face with someone else.

Drew closed up the back and put it back on. "Let's go before it gets late. I want to find this witch before dark."

They set off, and after a bit Scarlett spoke up. "Do you think we should have told Borane what was going on with the succubus?"

"I thought about it," Drew answered. "I mean, I did. I just... How do we know we can trust some random guy we met in the valley? For all we know, it was all a lie and he's actually another demon. We can't just trust anyone that comes along."

Scarlett nodded. "I guess I can see that. It is rather convenient to have met a Demon Hunter along the trail going to the witch's house when we have a problem with a demon."

"I was thinking that," Drew said. "Maybe he was what he said he was, and we made a mistake by not telling him. I don't know. We'll go back if the witch won't help us."

They walked until their stomachs informed them that it was time to eat something again late that afternoon. They found another small area where some trees had fallen and sat there for some of the food again. This time, they were silent, as they were getting tired of the trek through the valley. After they ate, they headed down the road again.

Just before dusk, they sighted a house up ahead. They both stopped, panting a little after a steep incline they'd just come up. "That must be her," Drew said.

"Borane said that she was the only other person in the valley," Scarlett added.

Drew turned to look at his sister and smiled. "You ready to try to get her help?"

Scarlett took a deep breath and nodded. "Let's go."

They approached the wood cabin and saw it looked exactly like what Borane had described. Fruit trees and berry bushes lined the house, and there was a garden full of herbs on the side of the house. The door was painted purple and had some sort of sprig of herbs hanging there. Drew and Scarlett approached and Drew knocked upon the door. There was no response, and Drew had to wonder if maybe the witch moved on or died. Then the door was jerked open.

"Whaddaya want?" groused a wizened and stooped old woman. She looked up and Drew saw she had eyes the color of steel, and her gray hair hung about her shoulders, long and stringy.

"Uh, I'm Drew. And this is my sister Scarlett. We came to ask you for help."

She looked between the two of them. "What kind of help?"

Scarlett spoke up then. "Our father has been manipulated by a succubus into forgetting we're his children, and forgetting our mother who was the love of his life."

The witch narrowed her eyes and nodded. "I might be able to help you," she muttered and stepped back, motioning with one wrinkled hand for them to come in.

Like Borane described, the interior was covered with shelves full of various things and strange masks making horrible faces. From the rafters hung bunches of herbs and flowers, for drying it appeared. The kitchen shelves were lined with bottles, and in the fireplace sat a large cauldron on the fire, bubbling with a greenish yellow liquid. She turned and sat at the little two-person table and looked at them.

"What are ya expecting from me?" she asked.

"We met Borane, and we didn't know if he was telling the truth about you giving him power to defeat demons," Scarlett said, crossing her arms across her chest.

"Aye, I did help him gain the power, it was not mine to give, though. The demon I summoned provided that." She looked at Drew. "You are not to be a Demon Slayer, boy," she said. "You don't have the ability like Borane did."

Drew blinked. "What? Why do you say that?"

The witch shook her head. "I can see people's souls, and how they connect to their destiny. Nay, you're not a Demon Slayer, boy. You may be a vehicle to allow your sister to gain a witch's power, though. Her soul reads the way a witch's does," she said, looking at Scarlett. "I could teach you to defeat demons if you're willing to learn the ways of a witch."

"Of course, I am!" she said, nodding. "I'll do anything to free my father from the evil that holds him!"

Drew felt strange at her words, but tried not to let it show. He didn't have the ability? What did that mean? And obviously, he didn't have the ability to be a witch, and his sister did, what good could he be if he couldn't do these things?

"Boy, I said, you two have a choice."

Drew shook his head and stared at her. "I don't understand."

"All magic takes a sacrifice to take root in the soul. I'm asking if you're willing to give something so that your sister will become a witch. Either that or she must give something so you may become the witch." The witch had a sly grin on her face.

"I can give something for her?" he asked, brow meshing together. "Why?"

"You're twins, so your souls are intertwined. One of you may make the sacrifice for the other."

Drew supposed that made sense. "What can I sacrifice?"

"I'm a witch who has dabbled in demons for a long time, but never had the ability to become a Demon Hunter. I was, however, able to learn to ensnare and bend demons to my will once summoned. That is how I was able to allow Borane to become a Demon Hunter, and over the years there have been others." She looked between them. "You say you have a succubus, and they are the most difficult demons to deal with because they are bound to an incubus. If you do not kill the pair at the same time, neither will die."

Scarlett and Drew glanced at each other. "So, how do we find the incubus she's bound to?"

"That's something only another incubus can tell you," she said with a shrug. "And the only way to get information from an incubus is to allow them to feed, and if the morsel is sweet and to their liking, they may part with the information of the other demon's True Name, which is what you need to summon him when you are preparing to kill his counterpart."

"Feed? Like on a soul?" Scarlett gasped. "I'm not letting Drew give his life so I can learn from you!"

"Oh no, the incubus doesn't want to feed like that. They don't have to consume their prey. No, it is much more... carnal." The witch said. "Now, I could teach your brother, and he would be able to learn it, but female witches are stronger just because of our natural connection to the ley lines of magic. But I will give you the choice. One of you will become of witch, the other will satisfy the incubus until such time as he is sated enough to give up the information we need."

Drew and Scarlett exchanged a glance. "Wait, so you want one of us to learn from you, and the other one is going to be demon food?" Scarlett asked.

The witch nodded. "That's the choice, now what will it be? I won't wait long for the answer."

Scarlett turned to Drew. "You're able to do this, Drew, I'll be the demon's sacrifice."

Drew shook his head. "No, she said you'll be stronger, you should take the witch's training. Besides, I can't let you do that."

"I don't want to see you sacrifice yourself, either!" She frowned deeply and glared at him.

"Look, the succubus things she's going to succeed in destroying our father. We have to have the most power behind us as we can, especially if we not only have to kill the succubus, but her incubus counterpart as well." Drew knew what his decision was already.

"I'll be the sacrifice."

"No!" Scarlett said, grabbing his arm.

"It's decided," the witch said, slapping her hand on the table and standing up. "Come, Drew."

"Where are we going?" Scarlett said.

"You aren't going anywhere. If you step foot outside this cabin, I will refuse to teach you, and your brother's sacrifice will mean nothing." She smiled. "I am not the kindest teacher, either."

Drew smiled as he followed the witch out of the room. He waved at her and he could see tears falling down her face. He wasn't sure what exactly this sacrifice would entail, but it didn't matter. If this was the path to get their father free of the succubus, then he would take it gladly.

She led him behind the cabin to a small building built of logs. She opened a heavy, banded wooden door and went inside. Drew hesitated, because a strange smell wafted out of it. He swallowed and followed her. Inside, she made a motion and a light appeared at the apex of the slanted ceiling. He could see now, there was a makeshift pallet on the ground, as if someone had slept in the room. The floor was concrete under it, and the room was perhaps ten feet tall, and around ten feet wide and twenty feet the other way. The walls were just the logs, and there was no window.

"This is a warded building," she explained as she pulled the pallet over to the side of the room, revealing a carved circle in the floor. Strange runes were all around the circle, and it looked smooth otherwise. "Nothing can get out that is summoned here, not physically or spiritually. You will remain here with the incubus until he is ready to give the information."

Drew nodded. "Uh, what do I do to tell you when he's ready to part with the information?"

"I'll know," she said with a nod as she began pulling herbs and a potion bottle out of her pocket as she began to speak strange words. Finally, at the end, she spoke loudly. "Hixas. I summon thee."

Smoke began to come from the floor, growing thicker and thicker until it was heavy and filling the circle. Then, the smoke began to fade, and Drew took a step back.

What he assumed was Hixas stood there. He was at least seven feet tall with broad, thick shoulders. His body was perfect, muscled and the skin was slightly red tinted. His eyes glowed red much like Gracelyn's had when she revealed herself to them. His body looked mostly like a human's other than clawed feet, the wings, and horns that graced his forehead. He wore a wrap around his waist and that was it. Drew's eyes were wide because other than being a demon, he was very attractive. He felt his mouth go dry as he waited for what happened next.

Chapter Five

The Incubus

For a moment, Drew stared at the creature before him.

"Why have you summoned me, witch?" he demanded.

"I have come to you with a proposition. A human to sate you, and in exchange the True Name of one of your brethren." For a frail old woman, Drew thought she had an extremely commanding voice when it came to the demon.

He scoffed and shook his head. "You know a true name is not freely given."

"And you know a human's sacrifice to do as you ask is rare," she responded.

Hixas snarled and looked toward Drew. "This is the human? He's a boy."

"He's old enough for you, an adult by human standards," she pointed out.

The demon's eyes fell on Drew, and he sniffed the air. "He seems to not be opposed to the idea by the smell of him."

Drew had no idea what that meant, but he glanced over at the witch. "I'm to be a sacrifice to him?" he nearly squeaked.

The witch chuckled. "I'm sure you'll be the happiest sacrifice there ever was," she muttered as she turned toward the door.

"Wait, you can't just leave me here!" he said, rushing to her.

She stopped and stared at him blankly for a moment. "Listen, you agreed to this, so you need to accept your fate. You're the sacrifice."

Drew turned back to him. "Is he going to eat me?" he whispered.

"I'll do more than eat you, boy," the demon chuckled.

Drew's eyes widened and he gulped audibly. The witch clapped him on the back. "Don't worry, you won't die. He's not going to kill you. That would defeat his purpose of being here. He can't enjoy his meal if you die."

Drew tilted his head to the side and stared at her. "What? That doesn't make sense."

"Boy, are you daft?" the demon asked. "I don't want a daft meal."

"He's smart enough," the witch answered. "Just be a good boy, and spread your legs for him."

Drew blinked, then he glanced at the incubus, and it dawned on him what kind of "meal" he was supposed to be. He moved to say something, but the witch was gone. He went to the door and realized there was no handle on the inside. It could only be opened from the outside. He put his hand against it and nearly jumped out of his skin when the demon placed his hands on his shoulders.

"You're trembling. Drew, that was your name?" he said in the low rumble of a voice.

"Um, yeah," he said, not turning around yet.

"You don't have to be afraid of me, Drew. Here, turn around, look at me," he said, and pushed a little on his shoulder to turn him around.

Drew turned, looking up at him, mouth drying as his eyes traveled up his body to his face. His eyes had stopped glowing, instead settled into a deep brown that looked like the depths of night. Kind of like Borane's eyes.

"Yes, you have a lover in mind, don't you?" Hixas whispered, reaching up a caressing his face.

Drew turned into the touch, sighing a little because he'd never been touched that way before. He reached a hand up and covered the hand on his face, and in his mind, it was Borane touching him. The room smelled sweet for some reason, and it was so comfortable in it. He wanted to feel more touches. He wanted to know what it was like to be with someone like Borane.

"Yes, there you are," he heard the deep voice say and felt hands on his hips, sliding his pants off. He didn't mind at all. "You're already like this? I haven't even touched more than your face," the demons said, and Drew felt him take hold of him. He gasped, bucking his hips forward, having never had someone else touch him like that. "Good, good," he heard.

Before he realized it, he was laying on the pallet. It was a little rough feeling but he didn't mind as he felt light kisses on the inside of his thighs. He wasn't watching, his eyes closed and his mind still envisioning Borane between his legs. Then, he was licking him, sliding his tongue down and into him. He arched, gasping as his legs flexed around his shoulders. How did that happen? He didn't care, and didn't want to care, either. The tongue worked inside him in such a way that he thought he was going to come undone at it. Then, he licked up to his cock, taking it into his hot mouth. Drew did come undone then, panting as the sweet smell took over his senses.

"Good, you taste wonderful, Drew. Are you still imagining your lover?" the demon whispered in his ear.

Drew didn't know when he laid over him, but he reached his arms around him, putting them under the wings across the incredibly strong muscles of the demon's back. For some reason, his arousal was back already. The sweetness was cloying, and he thought briefly that it might be a sickeningly sweet smell, but then the thought faded as quickly as it came. He felt him pressing against him and if he'd been more aware, he might have been afraid, but as it was he was imagining Borane still.

"It might hurt a little, Drew, but breathe through it," the demon said, and he felt him move.

He slid into him smoothly, and Drew gasped. It did hurt as his cock stretched him open. He had to be huge, he thought as he moaned as he continued to push forward into him. He had no idea how deep he was going to penetrate him, but it felt odd, but strangely good. He squeezed him with his legs and whimpered as he seemed to finish pushing into him.

"That's a good boy, you took it all so well," he said, stroking his hair. "Wouldn't your lover be proud of you?"

Drew saw Borane's face and imagined how he would look pushing into him. It was a beautiful sight. The demon pulled back and pushed in again, making Drew gasped and whine out loud as he felt the slick slide inside him. Then, he began to thrust back and forth slowly. Drew's heart was hammering in his chest, and he couldn't get a thought to stay in his head. All he could concentrate on was the feeling of being filled up with the demon's cock. It rubbed against something inside him as he thrust back and forth and he began to moan constantly, feeling an orgasm slam into him again.

"Oh, yes, there you go, give it to me," the demon whispered, still pounding into him. "Give me more, Drew. Give me everything you have."

To Drew's shock, he was aroused again. He didn't know how this was possible. He gasped, his lungs filling with the incredibly sweet smell in the room. He panted and didn't know how much more he could take as the scene was repeated several more times. He lost count how many times he came, and eventually he was laying on the pallet alone. He blinked wearily and sat up, completely nude now. He looked around, but he was alone. Where had the demon gone? Or had it all been a dream.

In his head, the demon's voice whispered. *I haven't gone anywhere. Not for long, anyway. I'm still here and will come back when I am ready to taste you again.*

Drew swallowed, running a hand through his hair. So, that was an incubus. He didn't notice the exhaustion as being anything unusual, but perhaps he should have thought more about the fact he could barely keep his eyes open.

* * * * *

Drew woke sometime later and heard a knocking on the heavy door. He blinked and realized there was an opening at the bottom of the door. He crawled over to it.

"I see you made it though your first time with Hixas," the witch's voice said from the other side.

"Please, can I leave now? I've done what you asked. What he wanted."

"Oh, you're not done yet, Drew," the witch said, and through the slot, a plate of food appeared. "I'll bring you food each night, and each day, you'll sate the demon. I don't know how long, so don't ask. It will end when he tires of you, I would say, but don't expect it anytime soon. You're the sacrifice, you didn't think it would be as easy as being fucked by a demon once?"

Drew stared at the plate of food. Part of him wanted to push it back out in anger, but he wasn't going to starve here. No, he was going to wait this out. Eventually she would let him out, and by then his sister would be a witch in her own right. He nodded to himself. He could do this. He could wait out the witch.

It turned out more time would pass before anything changed. He waited, ever patient, as the demon visited each day, taking what he wanted from him freely, because when he appeared, Drew wanted nothing but to satisfy him. It was strange, because afterward he didn't remember why he felt that way. He wanted to leave the rest of the time, but when Hixas appeared, all he wanted was to serve his every desire. In his mind, he still imagined Borane, and it was an ever more involved image as he went forward.

Each day, his energy waned more and more. It took a bit for him to notice this fact. At first, he'd be awake a lot of the day after Hixas left, but then it slowly began to change where he was sleeping through the time he wasn't there, until he woke each night to eat, then fall into another deep slumber until the sweet smell woke him again. The smell, he realized signaled Hixas was there, and no matter how deep the sleep, he would awaken immediately to his presence.

"You're a wonderful source of pleasure for me," Hixas said as he pushed into him from behind.

Drew, on his hands and knees, arched his back and moaned deeply as he began his rhythmic thrusting into him. He had done things with Hixas in so many ways, and he had done so much with him. He moaned as he began to speed up until he spilled on the ground below him. Only a few thrusts later from Hixas, and he was hard again and already well on the way to another orgasm.

"Humans are beautiful creatures," Hixas continued. "They are carnal in their base nature, and love to be pleasured. You're a wonderful example, Drew, a very amazing one. It's been weeks that I've fed on you, yet you're still able to awaken when I arrive. Such a rare treat for me."

Drew thought a little about that statement. Did that mean that his feeding on him was draining him, and that's why he was so tired all the time? What happened if he couldn't awaken when Hixas arrived, he wondered?

"I thought I'd never partake of a human soul again after the witch cursed me," Hixas continued. "I believed she would never summon me to the world again, and I would simply be without my favored treat."

So, it was the witch who had made it so that Hixas wasn't able to contact humans. Had she cursed him because she wanted to protect humans? Or had she cursed him so she had control of him? He might have been able to think more on it, but he was coming once again and his mind went blank for a while.

Some time later, he was awakening again, and he heard the knocking. He crawled to the door again, taking his empty plate from the night before. He took the new plate and pushed out the old one.

"You cursed Hixas." He said it simply, but with as much strength as he could muster, which wasn't much.

The witch chuckled on the other side of the door. "Of course, I did, Drew. Why else would he come when I summoned him?"

"Why?" he asked, frowning as his head tried to fuzz over again. The world was definitely blurrier now than before.

"I am not a demon hunter. My abilities are not to kill demons, only control them. You sister doesn't realize this yet, but she will as she is the perfect protégé. She will learn my ways, and she will answer to only me in time. Eventually, though, you will fade from her memory. I've already started sweetening her tea with an elixir to make her forget the past, including you and your father." The witch chuckled. "You will eventually die here when you are no longer able to sustain the drain on your soul."

Drew swallowed dryly. "You tricked us into this."

"Of course, I did. You didn't think I was honest? Power comes at a price. Your friend Borane found that out, as well. You sister will gain great power, but the price will be losing you and your father. It will fade and she will only know my words." The witch sounded so sure of herself.

"It won't work. Scarlett won't forget me and our father. You'll see. And I'll survive to see her destroy you." Drew didn't believe for a moment that his sister would forget him.

"You can't stop it. It has already begun. She's stopped asking about you already. And soon, she will forget you ever existed." Her voice was still sure of what she was saying. "And I will get the name of another demon. That is one more I can summon and control. Hixas, he will give over the name of the incubus that is paired to the succubus feeding on your father. Then, I will control her as well when I control him."

"Why are you telling me this?" Drew asked, wondering why she would reveal so much to him.

"Because you're going to die with the knowledge that I've won. That I've taken everything from you, including your life. I've taken your sister, and you'll die here, caught between ecstasy and pain, and you'll enjoy every sweet moment of it," she said with a chuckle again. "I will have become more powerful than I was before because of you and your sister."

"I don't believe Scarlett will fall for your tricks," Drew said weakly. He was already growing more tired as he sat there beside the door. He leaned against the door with his back and closed his eyes, just for a moment.

He heard the sound of birds when he next opened his eyes. He was still sitting against the door, the plate of food uneaten beside him. He blinked and looked down at the food. It was dried meat and cheese, so he slowly ate it. It wasn't like it would go bad. Strange, though, he really wasn't hungry anymore. He was so tired.

The sickly sweet smell began to rise once again as the smoke poured from the circle in the center of the room. Hixas, he knew, was coming. He swallowed the last of the food and wondered what he would do today. Everything was growing so blurry he could barely keep one day straight from the next. It was all so seamless sometimes. He didn't know when one day ended other than the plate of food that appeared at the door.

"There's my boy," he heard.

He felt tears slide down his cheeks. "Please, I can't do this anymore," he said. "You're killing me."

"I am," Hixas admitted. "I am eventually going to drain every bit of your soul from your body. I have been, bit by bit, and I'll continue until you have no soul left to drain. But you enjoy our time, do you not? You are happy when I appear?"

"I don't want to die," Drew said. "I want to get out of here. I want to see my sister, and I want to save my father. That's all I've ever wanted to do."

"I know. But you know, most humans never reach their lofty goals. You were never meant to save your father, Drew. You were merely meant to die by my hand. Now," he whispered, and the smell wafted over Drew, causing him to breathe it deeply. "Shall we begin?"

Chapter Six

The Witch's Training

When the witch came back in without her brother, Scarlett stood up and glared at her.

"Where's Drew?" she demanded.

The witch smirked at her. "He's the sacrifice. You know that. You need to worry more about your training."

Scarlett pursed her lips and shook her head. "If I complete the training, will I find out what's going on with my brother?"

"Of course," the witch answered. "Just do what you're told and learn the skills to defeat demons, and you'll know everything you need to know."

The witch went into the kitchen and started opening cabinets and pulling out things. She started setting them on the table and looked over at her. "Well, are you coming?"

Scarlett narrowed her eyes with suspicion but went to the table where the witch had sat down. She pulled out the seat and sat down across from her with the bottles and small boxes between them.

"The first step to learning the power of the witch is to know your herbs, oils, potions, elixirs, and salves. A witch's primarily duty is that of a healer." She picked up a bottle that shimmered and shined. "Learning the basics of making healing salves and potions is the first step."

"How is learning how to make healing potions going to help me kill a succubus?" Scarlett asked and felt irritation starting to grow. "Shouldn't you be teaching me about demons?"

The witch looked at her. "Do you want to learn the skills of a witch or not?"

"I do!" Scarlett said with a sigh. "I just want to understand why I have to take the time to learn this when I need to learn how to defeat demons."

The witch frowned. "Every skill you learn is a building block upon which another skill is built. You cannot learn to defeat demons if you do not know the skills to heal first."

Scarlett nodded slowly. She supposed that made sense. Things had to be taught in a certain order and it wouldn't do to try to ignore basic skills in favor of more complicated ones.

Over the next two weeks, Scarlett learned with the witch about healing, herbs, and everything to do with potions and elixirs. The witch would cook dinner each night, something rather simple with ingredients from her garden, and then she would take food to the back of the house to Drew. Scarlett knew nothing else of Drew other than he was back there and he was performing his duty to get the information they needed.

"I need to know about my brother," Scarlett said after she came back one evening.

The witch narrowed her steel gray eyes at Scarlett. "Your brother is alive. That is all you need to know."

"That tells me nothing!" Scarlett said, anger bubbling in her gut. "He's not just my brother, we're twins. We've done everything together since the day we were born. I'm being driven crazy wondering what his sacrifice is and why he cannot come back inside the house!"

The witch sat down at the table and began by pulling out a book. "Spells are the next step."

Scarlett wanted to scream. She wasn't going to answer her. What could she do but continue with what she was going to do. Maybe after she learned spells, she could see her brother again.

Four weeks went by, this time as she learned to command the base force of magic in the world. It was surprisingly easy for her to master, and just because she didn't entirely trust the witch, she didn't show all of what she could do. She would hold back, not allowing the full extent of her power to be seen. She had learned to shore up her mental barriers already, and it was extremely easy to let the witch think she could tell what she was thinking. In reality, she hid it from her.

By the time, she had masted the basic spells, she was growing more worried about Drew. Each day, the witch would take him food and bring back an emptied plate. So, unless she was taking the food and discarding it, Drew was eating what she took him. By this point, though, she knew that asking the witch about her brother was not going to yield an answer. For this reason, she decided to go check on Drew herself.

She had been preparing dinner lately, and she had gotten quite good at it. As she prepared the tea, she imbued it with her magic, disguising the spell and handing the cup to the witch. She could easily tell she suspected nothing, and thus drank the enspelled tea. They finished dinner and the witch took the plate out to the back building. She returned with an empty one and started to clean the dishes.

"Let me," Scarlett said. "I'll wash up. You look tired, maybe you need some sleep."

The witch nodded. "I am rather tired. Getting old, I suppose. I need more sleep than I used to."

The witch went to her bed while Scarlett washed up the dishes. She put away everything and dried her hands on the towel. She went into the witch's room and checked. She was deep asleep. She shook her and the witch didn't move at all. She smirked to herself and left, heading around back to find out what had happened to her brother.

The building behind the house loomed as she approached. She wondered why it was so big, but she supposed it had something to do with being where Drew was staying. She swallowed and went to the door, finding it firmly locked. She knocked on it, assuming Drew was on the other side. When it became apparent, no one was coming, she began to wonder if anyone was even in the building. Had the witch lied? Had she—the thought was cut off by a weak sounding "What do you want now?" coming from the base of the door.

"Drew!" she said, dropping to the ground to speak through it. "Open the door! It's me, Scarlett!"

"There's no handle; I can't open the door."

Scarlett blinked. He was locked in there? She swallowed. "I can't open it from out here without the key! What's happening? Why are you locked in there?"

"I'm the sacrifice, remember?" Drew said, and she knew his voice was way too weak. "I will never leave this place."

"I don't understand. She said I'd know what happened when the training was done."

"She doesn't want that to happen," Drew answered. "She is trying to erase your memory of me and Father. She told me that's her plan. She told me you were already forgetting."

Scarlett frowned and thought about that. She wasn't forgetting at all. Why would the witch say she was? Perhaps because she'd stopped asking about Drew. She thought about that. The witch never talked about Drew or her father, only about the training.

"She said she was using spells on you, and that you were her perfect protégé. She doesn't want you to defeat the succubus who is killing our father. She wants you to be her apprentice and I'm to die here when the incubus finally drains all of my soul." Drew sounded so defeated.

"No, that's not going to happen. I'm more powerful than the witch knows. I've been hiding my true power from her. I will learn all she has to teach, then I will kill her and come rescue you. I will not let her win and take my family from me." She nodded to herself to confirm this decision.

"Why aren't you forgetting, though?" Drew asked. "She's able to use spells you don't know, because I doubt she'll teach you the skills to defeat her."

"What she doesn't know is that I spend most my nights going through her spell books and her other books that talk about magic and how to use it. I haven't gotten to the books on demons yet, but I will as I learn from her. She doesn't know how much I've learned. I figured out how to read the language her books are in from how she's taught me from them. She doesn't realize this, and she won't. That's how I put her in a deep sleep tonight so I could come out here without her knowing," Scarlett explained.

Scarlett adjusted on the hard ground, as a rock was digging into her ribs. The night was very cold, and she could only imagine how cold her brother had to have been inside that room. Winter had come on in full, as they had been with the witch six weeks now. She wondered if Drew even had any blankets or anything in that place.

"I'm glad, but I don't know how long I can last, Scarlett," Drew said, still sounding so defeated.

"Drew, just hang on, for me. I promise I'll get you out of there. I will. You just have to hold on until I can defeat the witch. I'll even burn her body in that huge oven of hers, just to make sure she can't come back to life."

"That's good, Scarlett, very good thinking," he said, and she heard the smile in his voice for the first time since they had talked.

"Please, just hang on. You can do that for me, right?" she begged.

There was a pause, as if Drew was thinking. "I'll hang on for you. No matter how long it takes, I will hang on."

"Thank you, brother. I love you dearly, and I will free you."

"I love you, sister. I am waiting for the day I can see you again," he said, and his hand reached out the slot in the door.

She grabbed his hand and he squeezed. It was very weak, and his hand was like ice. She swallowed a lump in her throat because that grip meant he was not long for the world, and she knew that for sure. She squeezed carefully and let go.

"I must return. Be strong, my brother, and we'll get out of this."

"Defeat that witch, Scarlett. Do what you have to in order to save our father, with or without me." His voice was so faded and tired.

She got up, dusting herself off and hurrying back to the house. So, the witch was trying to manipulate her memories. She smiled as she closed the door behind her. She'd play the game, and she'd make her believe she was succeeding. For whatever reason, maybe because her bond with Drew was too strong, her spells were not working on her. It was just as well, because she was not going to lose to the witch. She peeked in to see she was sound asleep still, and went to the cabinet with the books again.

She cast the simple spell that she'd learned just by watching the witch open the cabinet. She selected the next book on the shelf and sat down to study once again.

* * * * *

Another five weeks passed before she sat in the kitchen, smiling as the witch talked about how well her training had gone, and that she had reached the end. Of course, the witch noted, there was more to learn, but she had learned all the basics of the witch's work, and so was able to go about the world and practice what she'd learned. Demons and their ilk had been the very last thing the witch had taught her, and during that lesson, she noted that talking about defeating her father's succubus never came up. The witch was utterly confident that she'd erased her memory of her family.

The witch opened the cabinet and selected the first book. It was one of the first that Scarlett had read at the very beginning when she learned how to open the cabinet. She smiled to herself. The witch was finally going to start revealing the deeper secrets of magic to her, but she already knew them all. She knew exactly what to do to defeat the witch.

"There are many secrets of magic," the witch began. "And I would like to start training you in them."

"I know them already," she said casually.

The witch looked up from the book. Scarlett was standing in the space beside the table. "What do you mean? I haven't given them to you yet."

"I've taken them. I learned many weeks ago what you are about to reveal. Alongside your learning, I've been studying the books in that cabinet. The secret knowledge you are about to impart I already know."

The witch shut the book carefully. "What do you mean? That cabinet is spell-locked."

"An easy spell for me to understand. I believe I'm rather good at this magic thing, you know. Because lots of things you said were difficult were very easy to me. Of course, I didn't tell you that. I acted the part I was supposed to act. And you never were the wiser, witch." Scarlett smirked. "Now, I'm going to give you a choice. Release my brother, or I will destroy you."

"Your brother?" the witch stood, eyes wide. "You cannot remember your brother."

"That's where you made a mistake. You thought your spells would work and I would forget, but I've forgotten nothing. I spoke to my brother, and he told me of your plan. And I did not allow it to happen. I used you for your teaching, and now you have the choice. Unlock that building, or I will unlock it myself over your dead body." Scarlet held her hands up in a defensive posture, energy already starting to gather near her palms.

"Never!" the witch shouted and struck.

An arc of red energy shot from her palm without warning. Scarlett, though, was ready, and the blue energy in her hand spread to form an effective shield against the attack. The witch snarled and struck again, this time sending the energy behind the shield. It didn't work because the shield morphed to block her every move. Scarlett smiled, finding the challenge enjoyable and easy to deal with.

"You bitch," the witch growled. "You will not defeat me! Do you know how many have tried? I've lived hundreds of years longer than the likes of you!"

Scarlett made not answer, only traded the shield for a growing ball of blue light, which she sent at the witch as she tried to strike with the red energy again.

Scarlett gasped, having given up the shield for offense, and fell to the floor in pain from the energy's strike. She gathered herself and stood, to see that her attack had knocked the witch completely out. She cradled her aching side and stood over her form. Could she really kill someone? She had no choice. If the witch was left alive, she would no doubt come after them.

She went to the great stove and opened it, pulling out all the shelves that were within it. She winced as each shelf was not light. She managed to pile all four on the floor. Then, she went to the witch and grabbed her under the shoulders to drag her to the stove. As difficult as it was with the injury, she managed to haul the small woman into the stove and shut the door. There was a lock on the outside, which now that Scarlett thought about it was curious. As was the ability to burn whatever was inside. She could only guess that the witch had used it before on her enemies. She turned the dials and walked away as the screaming began.

She got around back to the banded door of the building. She chanted the spell that would unlock any lock, and the door popped open. She rushed into the room and gasped because a demon was over her brother. He looked up and immediately the demon's name resounded in her head. *Hixas.* He stood and raised his hands and she chanted in the ancient language, ending it with a strong, "Begone, Hixas."

The demon screeched as he was sucked back into the smoking circle. She rushed over to the palate and kneeled beside her brother. He weakly turned his head toward her with his eyes hooded.

"It doesn't smell sweet anymore," he muttered, then seemed to pass out.

She swallowed and looked around for clothes for he was nude. She found what he'd been wearing all three months ago when this all began. She got him back into his clothes and he didn't move at all. She cupped his slack face and kissed his forehead.

"Dear brother, I will save you."

She knew enough to know that the incubus had been feeding on his energies for this long. Some people weren't strong enough and died quickly. It was obvious that her brother, like her, had been strong enough that he survived. She hoped she could do this as it was a day's journey back to Borane's house. She had to hope he was there. She knew a lot of demons, and she had read the demon books before she turned on the witch, but she didn't know how to help Drew.

She got him into the house again, and she noticed that the only sound was the roar of the fire inside the oven. She got Drew to the couch and covered him up. She walked over and turned off the oven. Now, it was silent in the house. She found a bag and packed it with meats, cheeses, and some bread for the walk to Borane's house. She went outside, finding a couple of long branches, and dragged them into the house. She went to the witch's room and grabbed bedding, and before long had fashioned a litter.

She moved Drew to the litter and positioned him on it. She then wrapped a blanket over it, tying it in place so it didn't move while she was dragging it. She wondered if there were some wheels anywhere, as she rummaged through the witch's room, eventually finding a small wagon. She sat down and disassembled the back and had a set of wheels and a small axel. She managed to use it under the end of the litter so it was framed and would roll when she pulled it. She smiled at her work. It wasn't pretty, but it would work.

She used some ripped fabric and wrapped the ends of the litter and tied it to body, so she would just have to walk, and would pull the litter behind her. She shouldered the pack and headed out the door. She thought about closing it, but then thought it would be amusing to see the animals take over the witch's house. So, with that, she left on her way back to Borane's house.

Chapter Seven

Healing Touches

Scarlett pounded on the door, hoping Borane was there. She'd done all she could with her healing magic, but it was obvious Drew was fading fast. She had no idea how to counteract what the incubus had done to him, as that was something that was not in the books that the witch had owned. She was growing frustrated until the door swung open and Borane stood there, completely naked, staring at her as she stood there in the dark.

"What are you doing here at this time?" he growled out. "It's after midnight."

Ignoring the nakedness of the man before her, she couldn't help the tears. "I don't know what to do. You're the only one who can help. He's dying!"

Borane leaned over and saw the litter being pulled behind her. He shook his head and gestured her inside. She followed, pulling Drew in and then unstrapping herself while Borane got into a pair of shorts near the bed. He came over where Scarlett was carefully untying the knots she'd made to keep him in the litter. Borane knelt beside it and helped free him from the cocoon of material she'd made. She went to lift him, and Borane put hand on hers.

"I'll get him," he said, his voice now much gentler and kinder.

He hefted Drew easily, and Scarlett held her breath as she watched him twitch a few times, and that was all. Borane laid him down on the bed and put his head to his chest. He listened for a few moments then stood.

"He's barely alive. What's happened to him?" he asked, his voice taking a harder edge as he looked at her.

"We went to the witch, and she said for the power to save our father, there would be a sacrifice, you know how it works. And she said we had a choice, one of us to attain the power, the other as the sacrifice. I think it had something to do with us being twins. Of course, Drew wouldn't let me sacrifice myself. He insisted that he do it. The witch said no one would die, or something, I don't remember exactly how she worded it now." She took a breath. "She did as she promised, and trained me, but I had no idea what happened to Drew. She would take food to the building behind her house every night, so I guessed he was alive."

She reached down and stroked his longer hair out of his face, and he made a small whimper at the touch. "One night, I used a sleeping spell on the witch to make her sleep so deep she wouldn't wake. And I went to the building. I talked to Drew through the door, and he told me her plan: to make me forget him and our father, and become her apprentice. She'd—she'd locked him in there with an incubus named Hixas. And she told him that Hixas would give her the answer to what the name of the incubus that was connected to the succubus that plagued our father. She said you had to kill them both at the same time, or neither would die. I don't know if that's true, because nowhere in her books on demons did it say that." She looked over at him desperately. "Is that true? Must you kill the incubus who is paired with a succubus for them both to die?"

Borane shook his head. "I've never heard as such," he admitted.

Scarlett felt her heart ache at those words. "She lied about everything, just to get me to become her apprentice."

"She never wanted an apprentice," Borane said. "She wanted you to become a witch, then she intended to steal your power like she has so many before you. But something happened, and what she had planned didn't work." He looked at her, brow creasing. "You are a remarkable young woman, Scarlett. You defeated her?"

"I did, then I put her in her oven, and set her to fire," she said.

Now, Borane's eyebrows shot to his hairline as he stared at her. "You did that? Did you know that only fire would kill her?"

She shook her head. "No, but maybe I did. I have more power than she knew, and she kept things from me that I found out for myself in her books after I learned to read the language."

"My goodness, in a short amount of time? You were there less than six months!" Borane looked truly shocked by this admission.

Scarlett stared at him. "It doesn't matter now, all that matters is you have to help Drew! He's going to die after that incubus fed on him for so long!"

Borane looked down at him. "Yes, he will die if nothing is done. You've already tried to heal him, I suppose."

She nodded. "Yes, and I'll do anything, even give up my mission to save my father, if you can just save Drew."

"You said the demon's name was Hixas?" Borane asked, walking to his small table and sitting down. "Was that his True Name?"

"Scarlett shrugged. "It must have been; I banished him using it."

Borane nodded. "There is nothing to be done tonight, Scarlett. Go lay down on the couch and rest. You've had a hard day."

"What about my brother?" she gasped.

"I'll worry about your brother. You need rest more than anything right now. He will be fine through the night; I'll ensure that." He nodded toward her. "I'll get the blankets for you."

She waited as he came back and carefully handed her the blankets. She took a look at Drew's pale face and had to trust that Borane knew some way to help him.

* * * * *

Borane watched over Drew throughout the night. He was tired, but he chose not to sleep, because there was no assurance that now, with the witch dead, that the demon wouldn't come to finish Drew's soul for good. Borane knew the demon Hixas. He'd helped her bind him to her will. He swallowed and glanced at Drew. Who knew that what he thought was a good deed would be turned on someone he wanted to help?

He knew the witch wasn't good. He chose to ignore this, though, because she'd given him the power he was able to wield now. Even that had been to her own benefit. She hadn't been able to bind Hixas without a Demon Hunter. So, when he came to her as a young boy, he'd fallen into her plans. He became the Demon Hunter she needed. She'd already made a pact with the elder demon, something that made that demon give Borane the powers he needed. He didn't want to think about what it could have been. He'd never heard the True Name of that demon, either.

Sighing, he glanced over at Drew. He was unnaturally still, and he knew that if he didn't do something, he would die. To have his soul fed on for that long, it was a wonder he was still breathing. Most humans succumbed in days, not months. For Drew's soul to have fed this demon for as long as it had, it was strong. The question, though, was his soul strong enough to survive now?

He stood and stretched, turning toward the room where Scarlett slept soundly. The girl was a powerhouse. To actually defeat the witch was a feat, but to manage to keep her brother alive as she dragged him all the way to his house, that was no small feat either. The fact that the witch saw in her the potential to become great was important, and one that Borane was not forgetting.

"Borane?" he heard from the bed.

He turned and saw Drew's eyes were open, droopy, but open. He was staring at him, a confused look on his face.

"Drew, glad to hear your voice," Borane said as he came and sat on the bed beside him. "I was worried when your sister brought you here."

"What happened? I thought I was dead."

"You almost were," Borane said, patting his hand through the blanket. "That incubus nearly succeeded in draining your life force away. How did you survive him for so long?"

Drew weakly shook his head. "I don't know. I just knew if I gave up everything to him, I was dead."

Borane frowned. "I don't understand, gave up everything to him? What does that mean?"

Drew sighed, even that a weak action. "Every time he came, something in me knew that if I let him, he'd take everything from me. He kept saying that he'd never encountered a human that could resist for so long. I guess that was a good thing, because I'm not dead."

"He said that? He said you were resisting?" Borane asked.

It seemed like such a small thing on the surface, but the idea that someone could willfully resist the pull of an incubus was unheard of in the demon world. The fact that Drew had done so for so long meant that perhaps they didn't understand the will of a human to survive. Just because it had not happened before, didn't mean it could not happen. Borane moved and brushed the hair off Drew's forehead.

"It was your face I saw," Drew said after Borane sat back.

"What do you mean?" Borane asked, frowning again. His face? How could that help him any?

"When he came to me, in my mind, I would imagine it was you. I would feel your touch, your lips, not him. I think it frustrated him, because he would get angry sometimes for no reason that I could see. But every time, I imagined it was you. I'm so sorry."

Borane shook his head. "What are you sorry for?"

"I used you," he whispered. "You kept me alive," he muttered the last and his eyes drifted closed. His breathing deepened, and he was obviously asleep.

Borane swallowed. He'd heard tales of people being taken by an incubus or a succubus and managing to survive for a while on the memory of their loved one. Never for months, though, that was completely unheard of. If Drew managed to use his image, that meant his feelings ran deep, even thought they'd only met briefly. What that meant was that the young man had a heart unlike any other Borane had ever met. And for him to be sorry that he used him to survive?

"What's going on?" he heard, and looked to see Scarlett had come over from the couch. "Why are you sitting there?"

"He woke up for a moment," Borane said.

"Aw, I missed it," Scarlett said with a definite pout.

Borane smiled. "I'm sure he'll awaken again. Right now, his soul is damaged by the incubus drawing it slowly away. It's simply amazing that he lasted nearly six months in those conditions. Most people last a mere day or two."

"The succubus has been with my father since we were babies. Maybe that's why?" Scarlett looked confused by that.

"Tell me about this succubus." Borane hadn't heard the tale as they had been unwilling to talk about it before.

Scarlett swallowed and nodded. "She married our father right after our mother died in childbirth. I think Father wanted to give us a mother, and he didn't care for who it was, really. They spent time together, like any couple would, but they slept in separate beds. I know that Father felt like he had to be true to our mother's memory, so he never embraced her as a wife," Scarlett explained. "Then, when we were old enough to leave, and Father convinced us to stay with him, she started trying to convince him that there wasn't enough food for us all over the winter this year."

"She wanted to get rid of you both, so she could have your father to herself," Borane said, nodding. It made sense. If the succubus wasn't succeeding in getting their Father to succumb, getting rid of the reminders of the woman he loved, such as her children, would help.

"Yeah, so she did something to him that made him do what she said, I know now the magic she used, I just don't know how she employed it, whether by his drink or by some other means. He took us to the river and left us there after taking us on a winding path to make us lose our way. But Drew had taken white stones and left them along the path. We followed them back, and when we got there, Father didn't know us anymore. We slept in the storeroom, which was filled with stores for the winter, and we confronted her when she came out there the next morning."

"That was a bold move. Confronting a demon isn't always the smartest thing to do when you don't know what you're doing," Borane said, looking at her.

"We couldn't not." She shook her head. "She said she enjoyed feasting on widowers who she replaced as the woman they loved in their life. And she said that she would feed off him as long as she could before she was done." Scarlett sighed. "It's probably too late for Father."

"Not necessarily," Borane said with a smirk. "Your brother got his gumption from somewhere. It is entirely possible that your father was able to fight off the same way your brother did. You are not the only one with power in your family."

Scarlett nodded and frowned. "The witch said that Drew was not worth anything, that he wouldn't become a good witch because he was a boy, and that he didn't have the talent to become a Demon Hunter."

"She obviously lied." Borane looked over at Drew's sleeping form. "If he hadn't had the power within him, he would have died. No, I think she saw his potential, and that potential was to outdo even her vassals, like me. She feared Drew, that's why she encouraged you to become the witch and forced him to choose to go to the incubus."

"But why? Why did she send him to the incubus?" Scarlett demanded.

Borane thought about that for a moment. What could have caused her to use Hixas in such a way? What was she getting in return from the demon? There had to be some exchanged.

"Nothing in our world comes without a price," Borane said after a few moments. "She was receiving something in return for giving Hixas access to your brother. I was there when that demon was bound to the witch's will. I helped bind him."

"You helped bring that demon here?" Scarlett asked, eyes going wide. "Why would you do that?"

"It wasn't my choice, and at the time, I was very young in the ways of the world. The witch had acquired the demon's True Name. As you know, she practiced some True Name magic, though she was nowhere near adept at it. She knew just enough to be dangerous. She knew how to summon the demon using the True Name, but that was all. Once it was summoned, she had no way to control it. That's where a Demon Hunter came in." He sighed a bit. "I wish I'd been less naïve, but she had helped me get revenge for my family by leading me to the demon possessed brigands who killed them. I trusted her then. That would change with time."

"So, what happened?" Scarlett sat in the chair near the bed and watched him carefully.

"She summoned Hixas, and I used my powers to bind the demon to her. By doing so, he couldn't enter the human world without her permission, and only she would be able to summon him. It was a simple binding charm, but strong enough to keep the demon to her will. Even though the demon was bound, though, a demon will not do something without an exchange of some sort. It was still up to her to convince him to give her what she wanted." Borane shook his head. "If only I'd know what she would do..."

Scarlett didn't speak for a long while. She just sat with her head down, probably thinking. Borane didn't know what she would feel about the situation, because in a way, Borane was at fault because he helped bind the demon. It wasn't something he was proud of, especially after the witch tried to kill him in his sleep the night he escaped her house. That had been a while ago, though, and he'd changed a lot since then.

"You couldn't have known. And like you said, you were young. But that doesn't explain what she was exchanging Drew for. What would she have been getting from the demon?"

That was indeed what was bothering Borane. There had to be some sort of exchange going on, and now that she was dead, the demon was no longer being sated. He was no longer bound and would likely come from Drew. He hadn't told Scarlett this, but it was likely he would appear before long to finish what he started, and with as weak as Drew was, Borane had no idea if he would be able to stop him from taking the last of his life.

Chapter Eight

Waking Up from a Nightmare

Drew didn't know where he was when he opened his eyes at first. Something had woken him up, and he knew exactly what it had been.

Hixas.

Ah, my sweet morsel, you yet live. I thought for certain you would perish after that sister of yours took you from me and sent me home.

He thrashed in his sleep, or what was more like being awake only unable to move. "Go away!" His voice came out in a harsh whisper barely audible in the quiet room. Something moved beside him but his mind wasn't on that. It was on the fact that Hixas had him in his grip already.

I shall feed upon you one last time, my sweet one. Your soul has been a wonderful tasting treat for me, but it is time for me to move on. I was interested in finding out how long you would last, but no, one more time will end your life.

"I don't wanna die," he whispered.

"Drew?" he heard, and he recognized the voice. Borane? He couldn't turn toward him, so deep in the demon's trap he'd fallen. "Drew!" the voice became more insistent. "You have to fight him!"

Oh, how cute, he wants you to fight me. Doesn't he know how weak I've made you? I've torn your soul under these claws of mine such that it'll never be healed.

Drew couldn't imagine how he was going to get free of him. He knew well, though, that unless the demon was to initiate physical contact, he couldn't drain the remaining parts of his soul from him. He had to depend on Borane, now, because he couldn't move no matter how hard he tried.

"Scarlett!" he heard. "Wake up!"

His eyes were glued shut, and he couldn't think of opening them. He wanted to see Borane, and he could well imagine his face in his mind. With his rich, brown eyes and his deep black hair, and the musky odor he had. Every sense was on fire and he wanted to feel his hands, and he wanted to know his touch; he wanted to know a real lover.

"Scarlett, it's Hixas. He's got a hold on his mind, but that won't be all. He'll come for him. He has to take him, has to physically touch him, in order to feast on his soul. We have to stop it somehow." Borane's voice was not really calm, and perhaps it was the fact that it wasn't that gave Drew hope he desperately needed.

They can't protect you from me. I'll take you, enjoy your body one last time as I consume the rest of your soul. Then, I'll leave an empty husk for them to find. No, you will not escape me again.

Drew's heart beat hard in his chest; he felt like a rabbit in a chase even thought he wasn't moving. He didn't know how to run, no matter how hard he tried, his body was frozen. He felt hands on him, smaller, delicate hands that had to be his sister, and bigger, strong hands that were Borane. He relished in being touched, even though the situation was dire. He had gone so long knowing only the touch of the demon that human interaction was precious to him.

He managed to open his eyes and found himself staring into the worried hazel eyes of his sister. She cupped his face. "Hey, Brother, we're going to help you," she said, insistent in her voice.

He wanted to tell her it was okay if she couldn't save him. He wanted to tell her that she had done everything possible to save him and he loved her greatly for that. He had no idea how she'd gotten to him, and how she'd opened the door and banished Hixas, but she had somehow. He blinked, turning his eyes toward Borane. Despite the dire straights he was in, his heart ached to look at the man. He was shirtless with a pair of shorts riding low on his hips, and he could so clearly see the v that went down his pelvic line. His mouth went dry from more than fear.

"He'll try to get him out of here," Borane said, looking around the room. "He'll have to come for him, but I'm not sure how."

"How did he find him?" Scarlett asked, standing up straight.

"An incubus, or a succubus for that matter, forges a connection between themselves and the victim of their attention. That connection allows them to track the victim no matter where they go. Hixas was bound until you killed the witch. She had bound him so that the only place on this world he could appear was in that building she had. When she died, the binding was destroyed. He was free to do as any other incubus, and he of course came for Drew to finish what he started," Borane explained. "He won't give up until he had what he wants."

"What do we do?" Scarlett asked, her voice weaker than it should have been, no doubt from fear.

"We protect him when Hixas appears."

"When will he appear?" she asked.

"Anytime," Borane answered. "He could appear at any moment, and we have to make sure he doesn't touch him. They can teleport with their victim, so if he grabs Drew, he'll disappear with him, and there is little telling where he will go."

Drew knew everything he said was true; Hixas had told him as much during their many times together. He delighted in revealing things to Drew because he was "marked for death" and wouldn't ever be able to tell anyone else. He swallowed, and felt his throat click dryly. He wanted to help. He wanted to defend himself. Then, a thought came to him. He suddenly knew how to defeat Hixas, and though it would put him in danger, he was not scared any longer. He knew what to do.

"Do we block the doors and windows?" Scarlett asked, and if Drew had been able, he would have snorted.

"Of course not, he'll just appear in here somewhere. Hopefully, he'll miss the mark and appear away from Drew. If we're really unlucky, he'll appear right beside him. It will just depend on how accurate the teleportation is for this demon. Some are good at it, while others aren't."

Drew knew it didn't matter. The demon was going to get to him, and he was okay with that now. He knew what to do, and he wished Hixas would simply hurry up and appear so he could get this over with. He wanted to be hugged by his sister again. He wanted to be embraced by Borane. It was a nice though, but he knew that the Demon Hunter would probably never embrace him the way he wanted. Still, he dreamed of the idea, and it was a pleasant dream to think of.

Drew turned his head to the side as the demon appeared. This would be it.

"Binding!" shouted Borane, and Drew felt a flutter of hope as a red ring surrounded the demon, binding his arms to his sides.

Something wasn't quite right, though. And he realized to his horror what his sister and Borane would have no way to know.

A string of unfamiliar words came from his sister, ending with "I banish thee, Hixas!"

Drew knew nothing would happen. The demon chuckled, and spoke, "I'm not Hixas."

Drew felt the world move under him as he was pulled from the bed and into a teleport. He grunted as he hit the ground of the all-too familiar building he'd been in with Hixas before. He looked up, the demon in his full demonic visage leering over him. He looked much different than the pleasing shape he took most of the time when humans saw him. He had deep red skin with black scales on his forearms and calves. More black scales sprinkled around his chin and forehead, and his fingers and toes ended in wicked black claws. His wings were spread wide, no doubt to look as intimidating as he could, and his horns were curling against his head, fully visible now.

"Ah, my sweet morsel, I will have all of you, now," he said, dropping to his knees and shredding the clothes from Drew's body.

The air hit his clammy skin, chilling him. For some reason, though, he wasn't afraid. He swallowed as he felt those clawed fingers scrape over his skin, leaving bleeding trails on his chest and then his hips and thighs. Hixas chuckled then growled as he pulled Drew's legs apart and thrust into him. Drew felt the sweet scent come over him, but for some reason, his head wasn't growing fuzzy anymore. No, he was remaining clear for some reason. He arched, acting the part that the demon expected when someone was under his spell. He reached his arms up, because he just needed him to lean over him and bring his throat closer.

Hixas smirked, leaning down, licking his forked tongue from Drew's belly up to his neck, leaving trails of fire among the scratches already there. Then, he put on arm around behind Drew and leaned down. Drew smiled because he had his chance. He reached up, lacing his hands behind the demon's neck for a moment. He had to wait for the right moment. He sensed the feeling of the demon drawing on his soul.

Through experience, Drew had learned a few things about demons, at least the incubus. Their skin was impenetrable by all implements, making them exceedingly difficult to kill. This hardened skin, though, had to be consciously done. They could relax the ability when in their home, in times when they felt safe, or times when their concentration was needed elsewhere. During the feeding sessions, Drew had noticed the suppleness of the demon's skin. When he felt the sensation of his soul's energy being drained, his skin became soft and easy to scratch. He'd experimented a few times, "accidentally" scratching him. The scratches remained after Hixas was done with him, healing very slowly on their own. So, he had a regeneration factor, but it was slowed when he'd been feeding.

So, which his hands around the demon's neck, he felt the skin was soft and supple as a baby's. He leaned up, kissing Hixas on the throat and smiled as he drew his hands as if to pull them down. Instead, with nails jagged and hard from months of ill care, he moved with incredible speed and sunk his fingers into the flesh on either side of the demon's neck. For a second, the whole world stood still. Then, he yanked both hands through the demon's neck, knowing that like humans, demons had arteries there that handled most the blood to their brains. They were not that much different, in the end.

Hixas jerked back, both hands going to his throat. His wings flapped uselessly as he stumbled a bit, blackish blood pouring from both sides of his neck, each marked with three long gouges.

"What?" he said, eyes starting to glow red. "No!"

Drew was so weak he couldn't move much, but he pushed up to lean on his elbows to watch as the demon dropped to his knees, his dark red skin turning lighter colored as his blood fled his body. After a few moments of tottering like that, he fell forward into the pooled blood under him, splashing it onto Drew's form.

Wincing at the acrid taste in his mouth from the demon's blood, he tried to reach to wipe it away. Instead, he only accomplished falling to his back again, staring at the ceiling. It had been close, he knew. The demon had almost succeeded. He wondered if Borane and Scarlett would find him. He hoped so, because he didn't want to die in the place of his torment. That was his last thought as consciousness slipped away completely, dropping him into the black velvet hands of darkness.

* * * * *

As soon as Drew disappeared from the bed, Scarlett gasped and glared at the new demon. "Who are you? Why are you helping Hixas?"

The demon, still bound in the circle of red. "I owed him a favor. But you know you can't kill me," he said, turning toward Borane. "Demon Hunter."

Borane growled. Scarlett knew as well as Borane that the skin of succubus or incubus was impenetrable unless they were feeding. They were stuck, because there was no way to destroy this incubus, and they did not know his True Name to banish him. They'd captured him, yes, but now the question was what to do with him.

Borane walked over to him and narrowed his eyes. "Where did they go?"

"It doesn't matter. You won't make it in time. He's already feeding on what little remains of that boy's soul. You may as well release me. I'll gladly leave, so you don't even have to worry about banishing me."

Borane glanced at Scarlett, then made a motion with his hand. The red ring dissipated quickly. The incubus snorted. "Thanks for the fun." Then, he was gone.

"We have to figure out where they went," Borane said, walking toward Scarlett. "Get packed up, we're headed out."

"Where are we going? We have no idea where he could have taken him. He could be anywhere!" she said, panic tinging her voice.

Borane, who was already filling a pack shook his head. "They're creatures of habit. My guess? He'll go back to the witch's location where he was bound. He'll return to the place he was using to torment him before."

"You think he'd be that obvious?" Scarlett asked, frowning as she packed her own pack, throwing food and clothes in it haphazardly.

"I do," Borane said and glanced over at her. "Ready?"

They headed out, locking Borane's house behind them. He paused to cast a spell over the house to protect it from outsiders, and then they took off at as quick of a pace as the two of them could handle. Borane, who was fitter than Scarlett, had to slow down for her, for which she was grateful. She was worried that she and Borane would be too late, and they were going only to retrieve her brother's body. They paused after a few hours and ate of the food they'd packed, then continued on as fast as they dared. At almost dusk, they came to the witch's house. Scarlett stopped, staring at it felt her heart beating heavily in her chest.

Borane turned to her. "Come on, we need to know."

Scarlett nodded and walked around behind the house. The building there loomed as they approached it, and they could see the door was open. In the dim light of twilight, it was hard to see anything.

Scarlett held her hand up and allowed a ball of light to form there as she came closer.

The light illuminated a form on the floor as they came through the door. Scarlett felt tears pricking her eyes as she went to it. She was equal parts afraid and curious about what happened. As she came up to the figure, she realized with a shock it was her brother, but he was covered in something that was almost black. He was nude, his clothes shredded around him, and rivulets of blood had dripped down his sides. She could tell nothing of where it had come, and she had no idea what the blackish substance was. However, to her amazement, he was breathing. It was light and shallow, but he was breathing.

"Demon's blood," Borane muttered as he came up beside her. "Did he kill Hixas?"

Scarlett kneeled, not caring about what happened to the demon, only that her brother appeared to be alive. She cradled his head, stroking his hair out of his face. The long, curly mess would need some help as it looked terrible, and barely appeared red in the light of the orb she carried.

Borane was looking around the rest of the building. He came back, shaking his head. "As near as I can tell, he killed Hixas. There are traces of brimstone on the floor, a sure marker for a demon's death. The black blood could only have come from a demon. I don't know how, but he's killed him."

Scarlett shook her head. "But he was so weak. How could he have possibly killed him?"

Borane looked thoughtful for a moment. "There's one possibility. He could have figured out that an incubus is vulnerable when they're feeding. He might have waited until he started to feed on his soul, then moved to kill him. I'm sure Hixas would have never suspected that a human would be strong enough to not only live so long while being fed upon, but also manage to move under the influence of his pheromones. Your brother is a remarkable young man," he said, kneeling and scooping Drew up in his arms. "Let's stay in the witch's house tonight, we can find something to put him in come morning."

They spent the night in the witch's house, one of them monitoring Drew while the other slept. Then they headed out at first light to get back to Borane's house. Borane rigged a carrier for Drew, easily strapping him to his back. Drew looked so small against the much larger Borane, and it was almost sweet to see Borane doing things so carefully with him. They stopped a couple times to eat, then got to the house around dusk. Once inside, they carefully put Drew in the bed once more.

Scarlett watched as Borane carefully washed him, cleaning his body of any blood. Then, as he was washing his face, he stopped and looked over at Scarlett.

"What if he ingested some of the blood?" he said, blinking at her.

"I don't know, it was all over him. What would happen if he did get some in his mouth? It's blood, right? Nothing bad?" she asked, beginning to worry all over again.

Borane shook his head. "It should be okay," he muttered, almost to himself.

Chapter Nine

A Demon Hunter's Birth

Drew opened his eyes, and it felt like they were made of lead. He was comfortable and warm, and he knew that he was safe. He wasn't sure how he knew that, but he was certain of it. He blinked and stared at the wooden ceiling of a familiar cabin. He heard light snoring next to him, and he turned to see Borane lying on his side facing him. So that's why he felt safe. Borane slept beside him. He glanced toward the windows and saw it was starting to turn light. It must have been close to dawn then. He wondered how long he had been asleep. The last he remembered was the rain of the demon's blood and then the world faded.

He shifted a little, feeling stiff as though he hadn't moved in some time and he nearly startled out of his skin when Borane's hand gripped his arm. He turned and was staring in his rich, brown eyes.

"You're awake," Borane said, his voice a very welcome sound to Drew's ears.

"I'm awake," he echoed. "How long has it been?"

Borane sat up and shook his head. "It doesn't matter; the most important thing is that you're awake."

That worried him. "Where's Scarlett?"

Borane sat up on the side of the bed and heaved a sigh. "She's been leaving before dawn every day, gathering healing herbs in the forest nearby. She'll return soon."

Drew watched as Borane got up and shuffled into the kitchen, and in a little while returned with a glass of water. "I'm sure you're thirsty."

Drew nodded, sitting up with great care because everything ached. He took the glass and sipped it at first, then began drinking the water faster. It was like ambrosia, it was so wonderful to feel the cool water in his parched throat. But it wasn't as parched as he would have expected if it had been a while that he slept.

"We've been dripping water in your mouth, hoping we were doing enough to keep you hydrated. We couldn't do much about food, but we tried mixing some herbs and giving them to you." Borane sat beside him and took the glass when he'd finished.

"Tell me how long," Drew insisted.

Borane reached out and took his hand. "Three months, thereabouts."

"Three months?" he repeated. "There's no way Father yet lives," he muttered.

"Drew, do not despair," Borane said, reaching over and taking his hand. "He may yet live. You survived the incubus. He may well have survived with the succubus."

Drew nodded. "I feel odd," he muttered, running a hand over his head, realizing his hair must have been cut while he slept because it was trimmed down to the way he normally wore it, with the curls around his head. "I can't describe how I feel though."

"I have a question, Drew. And I need to know the answer with absolute certainty."

Drew frowned and stared at him. "Um, okay."

"Did you ingest any of the demon's blood?" Borane looked very serious, and Drew was a little worried at that question.

He swallowed. "What if I did?"

Borane didn't say anything. "Did you?"

"It got in my mouth, but not much," Drew answered.

Drew's stomach dropped as Borane visibly paled. "It's a death sentence to ingest demon's blood," he said. "But you aren't showing the signs of being poisoned by the blood. I don't understand, even the smallest amount of demon blood should lead to death."

Borane looked over at Scarlett, who was still asleep. "Come to think of it, your sister also resisted the magic the witch used on her." He turned his gaze back on Drew, his brow scrunched in obvious confusion. "And you managed to kill an incubus despite the pheromones that normally incapacitate a person. Why?"

Drew shook his head. Now that he thought of it, he'd always been able to think, even when the sweet smell from the incubus was the strongest. Slowly, as he'd been exposed to it more, he'd been able to get used to it, and it seemed to lose the effect over time. Was that strange? He guessed it was by the way Borane was acting.

"I don't know," Drew said. "I feel fine."

Borane reached and grabbed both sides of his face, tilting his head back and widening Drew's eyes with his thumbs. He stared at him for the longest time, and after a bit, Drew needed to blink, so he swallowed and felt his muscles twitching in his eyes. Borane didn't seem to find whatever he was looking for, because he let go and stared. Drew blinked a few times and tilted his head.

"You're awful worried about me."

Borane frowned. "Why wouldn't I be worried about you?"

"I mean, I'm no one to you. Just some random, weak human that thought he could trick a witch into doing what he wanted. I didn't even tell you what I was doing when we met, yet you came to rescue me anyway when Hixas took me away. It was enough that you took me in when Scarlett brought me here, but why did you help?" Drew was truly curious about that.

Borane looked away, and Drew swore his face colored a bit, but maybe it was the light. "I just was being nice."

"You're not nice, you're a Demon Hunter," Drew said. "My father used to tell us stories that my grandfather told him about Demon Hunters. They're all self-centered loners who refuse help and refuse to help anyone dumb enough to get mixed up in demon business. They'll let you die, he said. Demon Hunters aren't nice."

Borane was still looking away. He shrugged. "I guess I'm tired of being alone."

Drew frowned, thinking about that. "Oh, yeah, since you can't touch a woman. That would be tough. But Scarlett, you know, she doesn't like men. Or women. Or anyone, for that matter. She doesn't ever want to get married or anything, and if you can't touch her, she wouldn't make for a good companion anyway."

"I'm not talking about Scarlett."

Drew blinked rapidly for a few moments before that statement set in. "Oh," he said after a while. "I mean, I'm not a fill in for a woman," he said, heart hammering in his chest at the implication. "I get wanting someone to replace a woman, but I'm not that. I want—"

"I don't want a fill in. I want you," Borane finally said, looking at him.

Drew didn't know what to say. "But you like women. That's why you were cursed never to touch one."

Borane sighed. "Well, I was young, and I thought that was the only option. I'd never been with a woman, and I was raised to believe that it was the only option. It was only after I began working as a Demon Hunter that I encountered other kinds of couples, and even groups, that were together romantically. I dreamed of perhaps finding someone, one day. But as you said, we usually work alone. But I'm tired of it. I want someone, and that someone is you."

Borane reached out and took Drew's hand where it laid on the covers, his larger hand dwarfing Drew's rather delicate one. "I know it's a lot, but there's something special about you, and I want you with me. I'll live a long time, because of the Demon Hunter's curse, so you'll leave me one day, but I want you until that day. I want you to be by my side."

Drew gripped his hand and pulled it up to his mouth and kissed his knuckles. "I want to be with you, too," he said, tears slipping down his face. "You'll take me, even after everything with the incubus? I'm far from pure."

"Purity is a manufactured concept," Borane said, reaching out and cupping both sides of Drew's face. "Let me kiss you."

Drew blinked as he drew close, nodding slightly. Borane closed the distance and brushed his lips against Drew's. His tongue flicked out, licking at the seam of Drew's mouth, and Drew opened to allow him entrance. Quicker than Drew expected, Borane moved his hands and embraced him, pulling him close to his chest, his tongue delving into his mouth, exploring every corner. Drew's shy tongue was dormmate at first, then he joined, twisting with Borane's and letting his teary eyes slip closed for a long time as they breathed heavily through their noses. It was the most sublime experience Drew had ever had, despite the fact that he'd done such things with the incubus. This was so different from that experience. This was in truth his first kiss.

They parted, and Borane leaned his forehead against Drew's. Drew swallowed. "Show me what it's like to be loved," he whispered to him.

Borane nodded, reaching down and slipping Drew's shirt over his head. He ran his hands over his chest, pausing to pinch and roll each nipple. Drew shivered at the touch. In his mind, he recalled such things that the incubus had done, but again, it felt different. This felt real, not some sort of foggy dream experience like the incubus.

"Lay back," Borane said, his voice quiet, and Drew knew he didn't want to wake Scarlett.

Drew did as he asked, laying back, and Borane began laying wet sucking kisses along his throat and chest, all along his body until he came to waistband of the pajama pants. Borane slipped the covers off him, and hooked his fingers in the waist, bringing the pants off his hips, then sliding his hands up from his ankles to the inside of Drew's thighs. Drew shivered again at the touch, because his cock was hard and leaking already. Borane didn't touch him, though, simply kept laying kisses everywhere else, teasing the sensitive flesh of his inner thighs as he parted his legs. He wanted to beg him to just touch him. But he didn't say anything because he knew his voice was not to be trusted. The last thing he wanted was to have his sister see him in this position.

Borane finally slid his hands up his cock and Drew bit down on his fist. He wanted to moan, and he did somewhat against his fist. Borane stroked him a few times, pausing to play with the tip and then he drew a damp finger down underneath and began probing at his entrance.

"You're twitching," Borane muttered. "Do you want this so badly?"

"Um-hmm," he hummed against his fist.

"Hmm, such a needy boy," he said as he slipped finger inside him.

Drew let out a sigh and thrust his hips upward. His eyes rolled up a little and he couldn't believe how impossibly good Borane's touch was. After months of being used by the incubus, he had never felt like this. He swallowed an overabundance of spit in his mouth, and tears squeezed from his eyes from the exquisite pleasure he was feeling.

He heard Drew spit in his hand and he didn't watch, but he knew he was slicking himself. He sighed again as he pulled his finger out and something larger pressed against him. Borane's hands were on his bent knees and he began pressing forward, breeching him easily. Drew moaned, unable to keep his voice completely in as he worked his way deeper and deeper until he felt their bodies meet.

"You feel so good, Drew," Borane said, his voice still quiet but it was obvious he was struggling to maintain composure. "It's like sliding into silk, and you're squeezing me so tight. I think you like the feel of me inside you. Do you, Drew?"

Drew moved his hand, reaching up as Borane leaned over, pulling his body close. He whispered in his ear. "You feel like you complete me," Drew said as quietly as he could. "It feels right, like this is what is supposed to be," he continued. "My body will know your shape, and no other will ever replace you in my heart and soul."

Borane nodded, his head against Drew's. "That's it, my boy, no one else can ever make you feel like this."

Borane began a slow rhythmic thrusting, and it nearly sent Drew off. Not only was his body being stimulated from the inside, Borane was laying over him and his cock was trapped between them, each move sending him closer and closer to the edge. He panted and gripped Borane's strong body, wrapping his legs around his waist as his thrusting began to increase in force as well as growing faster. Drew raised his hips to meet him, moaning softly in Borane's ear.

"Oh, that's it, my boy, my beautiful boy, moan for me," Borane said as he started to thrust hard enough that the bed was shaking a bit.

If Scarlett was awake, she was surely getting an earful, Drew though as he let his voice go, still trying to keep it low as he could. He couldn't hear the sounds he was making as Borane thrusted harder and faster. Drew was panting between moans and now and then Borane would quiet him with a kiss for a while, and the clashing of teeth and tongue was just increasing his need to reach the heights of pleasure.

Drew couldn't wait, and began to whimper at the effort to hold back his orgasm. "I need-need—" he gasped out.

"Come for me, my beautiful boy. Spill your pleasure for me, show me how good you feel," Borane said.

The words were enough to send him over the edge, his eyes rolling up and back arching as he came between them. His head filled with white noise, and he barely felt as Borane's cock throbbed inside him, filling him with his essence. He clung to Borane's body, and Borane embraced him in return with one arm while he stroked his head with the other.

"That's my good boy, my wonderful boy," he said in his ear.

It seemed the world faded for a while, and when Drew came back to himself, Borane was holding him and laying beside him. He felt like his mess had been cleaned somehow, but he didn't remember it. He clutched Borane against his chest, his heart beating slower just from his presence. Borane was stroking his hair and speaking words of encouragement, calling him his beautiful boy and other wonderful things.

"I love you," Borane said without warning.

Drew smiled, his head buried in his strong chest. "I love you too," he answered, and he truly meant it.

* * * * *

Drew woke up sometime later, and Borane had left the bed. He sat up and saw him and Scarlett sitting at the table, talking over some papers. He got up, noting that his clothes has been replaced. He wandered over to them and sat down beside Borane and across from his sister.

"Good morning, sleepy head," Scarlett said, smirking at him.

"What are you two doing?" he asked, reaching over and pulling one of the papers toward him. It was a map with a path marked out on it leading out of the valley.

"We've still got to save Father," Scarlett said. "If the succubus still has him, we have to release him from her hold."

"How can he still be alive? It's been so long..." Drew asked.

"You survived," Borane pointed out. "I am sure there is more than a small chance your father yet lives."

Drew supposed that was true. Apparently, it was a big deal to last as long as he had with an incubus. And even stranger that he was able to kill one like he did. He shrugged and got into the discussion of what they were to do.

By the end of the day, they'd decided a plan of action, and intended to set out the next morning to get back to their cabin. It wasn't a terribly long hike, but it was enough that they needed a couple of days' worth of supplies. They packed three bags, each with jerky, nuts, dried fruits, and an interesting flat bread that Borane knew how to make which stored easily for long trips. Borane himself packed a few bottles of some sort and strapped a long dagger to his hip. Scarlett packed a lot of bottles and small bags of herbs and various oils. She also packed a large book with a ragged cover. It was obviously well read and well used.

After Scarlett had gone to sleep that night, Drew moved to lay with Borane again, once more trying to remain as quiet as possible, but not succeeding as well as he would have liked as Borane took him from behind, driving him into the bed with every thrust. He left a bite mark on the back of his forearm from the effort to stay quiet. Once more, they slept in each other's arms until dawn's light awoke them from their slumber.

They ate breakfast and set out. Along the way, Scarlett told them about various herbs, flowers, and trees they passed. Borane talked about things he'd done, demons he'd fought, and people he met. Drew was mostly quiet, as he had not experienced as much as Scarlett and Borane. He didn't want to talk about Hixas and that experience anyway, and he only wanted to go through with killing this succubus which had their father enthralled.

As they left the valley, Drew looked back down into it and sighed. Who would have imagined that such things would occur? They were driven to go there by terrible events, and had suffered, but also changed into something greater than they were. Scarlett had become quite a powerful witch, though, and he had been nothing but a victim. He swallowed. He had survived, though, so he supposed that was something. Still, he felt so powerless in the whole situation.

Borane put a hand on his shoulder. "You okay, Drew?" he asked, frowning a little.

Drew put on a fake smile. "I'm okay, love," he said. "We should keep moving," he pointed out and hiked ahead.

Borane followed him and just before nightfall, they came out of the woods near their house. The lights were on, so it was obvious that someone yet lived there. They waited in the wood, and watched as their father came out and smoked his pipe. So, he did live, they thought. Then, the succubus came out and wrapped her arms around him. Drew felt anger build in his gut, but more than that, he felt something else. Something unfamiliar. How dare she touch his father?

"Wait," Borane said. "It is no good going in the dark. We camp, and come back in the morning."

Scarlett and Drew both nodded, and they retreated a little way into the wood and made a camp for the night, without a fire, but ate and got into their sleeping bags. Drew got as close to Borane as he could and slept fitfully through the night.

Chapter Ten

A Succubus Falls

Drew jerked awake when he felt someone shake his shoulder. He blinked and stared up into the hazel eyes of his sister. He sat up, running a hand through his hair. He saw Borane had already packed up.

"Pack up after you eat," Borane said, nodding at him. "We'll leave our packs here in the brush other than what we need to take with us. We'll wait for the right moment, when she's feeding from him, then we'll attack. Remember, the skin is impenetrable unless they're feeding."

Drew nodded, getting up and rolling the sleeping bag up. He put it away and sat down beside Borane on the fallen tree. He ate quickly, enjoying just being close to Borane and his sister. It was almost like they were a little family. Now, they just had to get their Father out of the demon's clutches.

"Ah!" he said, wincing and putting a hand to his lip which was bleeding.

"What happened?" Scarlett asked, frowning as she looked over at him.

"Bit my lip," Drew muttered, dabbing his sleep against his mouth. "Weird, never done that before," he said.

Borane glanced at him, a curious look on his face. "Just eating too fast; you're anticipating saving your father."

"I guess," Drew said, still a little bothered as he ran his tongue over his canine which felt sharper than it should. Maybe he broke it or something, he said, shaking away the thought. He couldn't worry about that right then.

As the dew dried on the grass, they went back to the edge of the wood. Their father was sitting on the small porch whittling something. He enjoyed whittling, something he'd always done. There were little statues all over their house that he'd made. Drew felt a strange sensation in his hands, almost like a tingling in his fingertips. Such a thing could not be of great concern right then. He had more to worry about than that.

"You okay?" Scarlett asked, turning toward him as they crouched behind the brush.

"Yeah, I'm good. There she is," he whispered.

The succubus—Drew wouldn't use the name she had used—stepped out and sat beside their father, and suddenly, a rage unlike any other settled into Drew's stomach, and he was moving before he thought.

"Drew, stop! What are you doing? You can't go now! We have to surprise her!" Borane whispered harshly, reaching for him.

Drew shook off his hand and walked out into the clearing around the house, and Scarlett and Borane both followed. Drew knew this wasn't the plan, but he intended to confront her no matter what. He may not have been a powerful witch like his sister, or a Demon Hunter like Borane, but he could at least do this.

"Demon!" he said as he came up to the house. "Release my father!"

The succubus looked up, seeing the three of them. "Oh, you're back," she muttered. "Who are you? My husband has no children."

"You are a succubus, and you've enthralled him. Father! Break out of the spell she's put you under!" Drew balled his hands into fists and glared at her as Scarlett and Borane came up on either side of him.

She chuckled. "Not going to happen," she said, standing and walking down the stairs. Her walk was confident and she stepped lightly. She turned to Charles and smiled. "Rest, my dear," she said, waving her hand at him. As if on cue, their father's head drooped and she stepped closer.

"You think bringing a Demon Hunter will help you? If you were smart, you wouldn't have revealed yourself. You know the only way to kill one of us is to wait until we feed, and now that I know your plan, you can't do that." She smiled, teeth sharp and wicked as she stared. "Truly a stupid move. If you were smart, you would have remained hidden."

"Let him go," Drew said, and he felt that strange sensation building, his fingers nearly burning as well as his mouth. He didn't know what was happening, but he wasn't going to worry right then. "This is your warning. We will destroy you."

She laughed then. "You can't destroy what you can't pierce! My flesh is like iron compared to that little blade your Demon Hunter friend carries! Didn't he tell you? Killing one of us takes baiting us, and usually our victim doesn't survive it. They don't care, they only care about killing the demon they're after!" She smiled, walking up to Drew and stroking his face. "You're too young to understand, child, but there is nothing you can do now. Until I die, your father is under my control, and I'm going to make you watch as I drain what's left of his soul."

She turned and walked over to his slumped form. "Normally, I'd feed, but I think I'll just release his soul, and then it'll be over, and there will be nothing you can do."

Drew blinked, the rage boiling over into something else. He smiled, and the burning in his mouth was relieved suddenly, and he glanced down and realized his nails had grown into black talons at the tip of his fingers just like the ones Hixas had on his fingers. What was this? He ran his tongue over his teeth and flinched as he nicked his tongue on one of them, as they'd grown long and sharp. He stepped forward and took the steps quickly, grabbing her and with strength he hadn't know he had, he pulled her away and down the steps.

"Drew?" Borane asked, frowning.

Drew turned toward him as the succubus got to her feet, turning glowing red eyes on him. Her own talons had extended and her body was turning red as she came toward him.

"You dare touch me!" she shrieked.

Behind him, Drew didn't see his father raise his head, eyes open and watching the scene. Instead, he stepped forward and swiped her face. She jerked and put a hand to her cheek, which was bleeding from four deep gouges.

"What?" she gasped. "You cut me!"

Drew smiled, revealing the sharp teeth in his mouth. Before she could recover from the shock, he reached out and gripped her throat, nails digging into her neck on either side.

"I'll let him go!" she said, red eyes wide. "I'll leave you be, just let go!"

Drew stared at her, his own eyes glowing red. "No," he said and ripped his talons through her throat.

She gasped, gurgling as she began to bleed out. She put both hands to her throat, attempting to stem the flow of blood. It was a useless action, as nothing could stop it at that point. She dropped to her knees, any words dying on tongue as she crumbled to the ground, falling into a pile of dust as she died.

Everything was quiet for a long time as Drew stood over her dead body. He looked at his bloody hand, the talons gone, now, replaced by his own human nails. He ran his tongue over the blunt teeth he had expected to find in his mouth. He blinked, turning around to see he was being stared at by three set of eyes. He flexed his blood hand, looking at his father now.

"The demon blood," Borane said after a few tense moments. "It didn't kill you. It changed you. It gave you demonic abilities, but how? You haven't made a pact with a demon. I don't know how this could be."

Drew's father stood, walking down the steps to where Drew stood. He blinked rapidly for a few moments, then he grabbed him in a hug. "My son," he whispered.

Scarlett came up, then, and as soon as Charles let go of Drew, she embraced him. "Of Father, I'm so glad she didn't drain your soul!"

Charles hugged her for a while then let go, putting a hand on her shoulder, and putting the other on Drew's. "She tried, but she didn't know what she was dealing with."

Borane frowned, staring at Charles. "What do you mean, she didn't know what she was dealing with?"

"My grandfather was a Demon Hunter," Charles said, looking at Borane. "My father chose not to follow him and become one, though his brother did. It was my great-grandfather who made the pact with the demon. Only the person who makes the pact carries the curse, their children inherit some abilities, though if they wish to become a full

Demon Hunter, they still have to take a curse." He turned to Drew. "I've never seen anything like what Drew did."

Borane frowned. "What's your last name?"

"Chambers," Drew said, looking at him. "You know that name?"

"I do," Borane said, looking at Drew with amazement. "The first Demon Hunter I trained with, the one who guided me through those first days, was Cameron Chambers."

"Cameron was my grandfather," Charles said, frowning. "You've gained the curse, and with it longevity."

"My curse is that I cannot touch a woman," Borane said, glancing at Drew. "But I found I don't need women to complete my life."

Charles tilted his head to the side, and Drew felt his eyes on him and a blush lit fire to his cheeks. "I see," Charles said. "And what gives my daughter such steel in her spine to approach a succubus face-to-face?"

Scarlett smirked. "I met the witch in the valley, and she trained me."

Charles frowned and shook his head. "That witch is evil. She trains no one, at least no one that leaves that valley. How did you manage to do that?"

Borane smiled. "Your daughter inherited some blessings, herself. She was to be the witch's next victim, her power to be stolen like all others who the witch takes in to train. The witch didn't expect her to turn on her. You daughter defeated her with magic, then roasted her alive in her great oven."

Charles frowned, shaking his head. "That's... Well, that's amazing." He looked at Drew. "And how would you have acquired demon's blood?"

"The witch made us agree that one of us would be a sacrifice," Drew explained. "I wouldn't let Scarlett do it, but she locked me in a building with an incubus. He fed on me, thinking, like you, I was enthralled, but eventually I was able to figure out that when he fed, his skin became supple. I guessed they were vulnerable when they fed, so when he fed on me, I ripped his neck open with my nails, and blood got into my mouth. I didn't know it was a big deal until Borane told me it was," he said, looking over at Borane.

Charles shook his head. "The blessings from your grandfather gave you the power to survive," he said. "Just like me, with the succubus."

"Were you really enthralled, or were you pretending to fool her?" Scarlett asked, turning toward him.

Charles smirked. "Well, that's another tale."

Borane looked a little out of place, Drew thought as he looked over at him. He stepped over and grabbed his hand. "What's wrong?"

"You'll want to come back to your father," Borane said. He looked up, meeting Drew's gaze. "I mean, that's okay. Now that the succubus is gone, I'll go back home."

Drew frowned and put his other hand on his hip. "Don't think you're getting out of this that easily," he said.

Borane blinked. "What do you mean?"

Scarlett snickered. "You honestly think we can just go back to living a normal life after everything that has happened? I sure can't. I want to learn more about demons and how to kill them!"

"And I just found out I can pierce demon skin!" Drew said. "We're not just going to go live in a cabin in the woods and cut trees for the rest of our lives. We're going to hunt demons."

Borane tilted his head to the side and looked at him. "Hm, a brother and sister demon hunting team without a curse. That will be something to shake up the Demon Hunter ranks."

"Not just a brother and sister," Charles said. "I think what my kids are saying is that we can together make a formidable team."

"You too?" Drew said, looking at his father.

"Well, I may not have any fancy powers since I didn't take the curse, but I have all my grandfather's books and journals from his Demon Hunting years, and I also have a lot of knowledge just from what was imparted to me by him before he died." He shrugged. "I think I could be useful."

"A team? Demon Hunters work alone," Borane said. "I mean, I've never heard of such a thing."

"You've never heard of someone gaining demon powers without a curse, either," Drew said.

"Or a witch that can overtake another one three times her age," Scarlett added.

Charles looked at Borane. "A family team. And sounds like you're a member of this family now, Borane Withers."

Borane blinked and stared at Charles. "How did you know my last name?"

Charles winked at him. "I told you; I have my grandfather's journals. You were named in them, and I couldn't think of another person with such an odd name as Borane. I mean, it's definitely not something you run into every day."

Borane shook his head with a bemused smile on his face. "Wow, I don't know what to say. I mean, I've never thought of doing this with others, and who knows how long Drew and Scarlett have, after all they've attained powers unknown to me. They may yet live as long as I'm cursed to live."

"You always wanted a family," Drew said, feeling his face heat up. "We can have a family if we want."

Borane frowned and looked at him. "I don't understand. I can't have children with a woman."

"There are many children who need parents out there," Charles said, nodding.

Scarlett looked thoughtful. "No, I'll give you a child, to keep our bloodline running."

"What? You don't like men!" Drew said.

She shook her head. "There are other ways to get pregnant, stupid boy. I don't need a man to get knocked up. I just need Borane's seed, and we'll have a baby that is as close to being yours and his as possible. I'd be willing to carry a baby for you to raise. We'll just have to hope it isn't a girl!" She looked at Borane. "Otherwise, Borane can't help take care of it!"

They all chuckled at that thought, and there was a good feeling in the air. They eventually all went inside and shared a drink of some very old whiskey that Charles had been saving for many long years for the right moment. This moment was as right as any other.

Epilogue

The Next Generation

"Russel Withers!"

The fifteen-year-old boy turned and stared at his father and his dad. He bit down on his lip and sighed. He put down the book he'd taken from his aunt's cabinet. She always told him he could read what he wanted, but he hadn't actually asked if he could borrow this particular book.

"Yeah, Dad?" he said, looking at his smaller, red-headed parent.

He'd taken after both his parents, having his dad's bright red hair, and bright green eyes. Physically he'd taken after his father, though, standing six feet almost at fifteen, and having thick, heavy muscles like him. He had gotten his aunt's inquisitiveness, and he was a voracious reader. He'd already picked up the basics of healing at his aunt's tutelage, and had gotten in trouble several times for attempting other spells.

"You know as well as I do that you didn't ask Auntie for those books."

"I'm sorry, Dad, Father, I just—" he started.

"No!" his dad said, frowning. "No excuses! You march right back in there and put them back on the shelf they came from and apologize for not asking first!"

Russel sighed. "Alright," he muttered, getting up from the outdoor table he was seated at.

He walked past his dad, who was sternly watching him, while his father looked rather amused at the whole situation. He walked around to his aunt's side of the double house they lived in. He lived on the right side of the building with his dad and father, and his aunt lived on the left side of it with his grandfather. It had originally bee a sparse, one room log cabin when his father built it initially, but a bit before he was born, they had rebuilt the place for all of them to live in.

He opened the door, hoping to not meet his aunt along the way, but as he was putting the books back into the locked cabinet he felt eyes on him.

"You learned the unlocking spell," he heard behind him.

He turned around, a sheepish look on his face as he stared at his red-headed aunt. She had both hands on her hips and a slight smile on her lips. Her hair was pulled up in a bun, and she wore a pair of glasses that had a chain connecting the earpieces around the back of her neck.

He looked back at the cabinet, shutting the door and muttering the reversal of the unlocking spell. There was a click as the lock engaged. "Um, yeah."

"What am I going to do with you?" she said with a great sigh. "You know those advanced books need to be read after you're finished with the right lessons. Reading them now may teach you things, but you can't truly understand until you learn other skills. Remember, it's like building a castle. You can put the spire on the tower until you build a foundation and build up to it. I know you want to know the stuff about the demons so you can go hunting with your parents, but you have to be patient."

"I just don't understand why I can't do it yet!" he said, frowning. "You get to go wherever you want and I am stuck here with Grandfather going over maps and plans!"

"That's important, too, you know," she pointed out.

Russel sighed, knowing she was right. He wanted to get out there so bad, though. "I want to take the curse, too."

"That's a talk with your parents, now, get out of here and go back to your side! I'm sure they'll want to talk to you about this."

"I know," he muttered and headed out, waving at his grandfather who was sitting in the living room reading the paper from Sapphire City.

He headed back around to their side, kicking a rock as he want. He didn't like being in trouble, but he felt like he could do so much more than he was already doing. He opened the door and went into the house and saw his parents setting at the table, staring at him as he came in.

"Look, I'm sorry. I just really want to go with you demon hunting, you know? I like helping here, but I'm ready! I know how to fight, and I know a lot of spells already!" he said.

"You obviously know the locking spell," his dad said.

Russel nodded. "Yeah, I figured that one out."

"Come here and sit for a minute," his father said.

Russel dragged his feet as he went over and sat down. He slumped in the chair and ducked his head, ready for the lecture that was to come. His parents never yelled, in fact, they never got angry at all, but boy could they lecture. And they always were right, and he knew it, but it was still a pain to have to listen to it.

"Son, I know it's tough being your age and wanting to get out in the field," his dad said. "And you know that we understand that. But we want you to be safe and ready when you go out there."

"No one is going to hold you back when the time is right," Father said. "We've got a lot more experience than you right now, and a lot more knowledge."

"I want to take the curse," he said.

"Wait, where did this come from?" Dad asked, brows meshing. "You're learning from your aunt. You want to do both?"

Russel nodded. "I've only been studying for two years with her, and I am almost ready for the demon level books. I want to take the curse and learn from Father."

His dad and father exchanged a glance, and Russel didn't know what that glance said. He swallowed and waited for what he thought was going to be the squashing of his dreams.

"Okay."

He looked up at his dad. "What? You're going to let me take the curse?"

His father shrugged. "It's not our decision, son," he said. "You are the one that makes the call on what you do with your life. I've never seen a Demon Hunter witch, but that's not to say there can't be one. They're very different skill sets, are you sure this is what you want?"

Russel nodded. "It is. I want to do it. I can do it."

His dad still looked a little skeptical. "Taking the curse is a big deal. You have no idea what the curse will be until it's done. You could end up like your father and never be able to touch a woman, or like your great grandfather, and be cursed to need to drink blood to survive."

"I know," Russel nodded. "I can handle whatever it is."

"Well, it is your decision, but let's not make it today. It's a decision for a man, and you're not there yet," Father said, a stern look crossing his face.

"But Father!" he said with a whine to his voice.

"My one rule for taking the curse is that you must be a man. You are a teenager. When you turn twenty, you can make the choice for yourself." He looked like there would be no argument on this issue.

Russel acquiesced. "Okay, but when I'm twenty, you'll help me? And until then I can train in the other skills to be a Demon Hunter?"

Father and Dad both nodded. "You'll learn to fight, hand to hand and with the long knife. Then, we will get you your own inscribed long knife blessed by your aunt and imbued with magic." Dad smiled. "We're both very proud of you, Russel. Just know that. I know we're hard on you sometimes, but it's because we love you very much and we want to see you do things the right way. It's a dangerous business, this one we're in."

Father put an arm around Dad. "And just know that we'll always be with you, through the whole thing."

Russel gave them a small smile, feeling a little better. It wasn't a no, but it was a wait five more years. He knew he could learn a lot in five years. He could become the very first Demon Hunter Witch.

About the Author

BEVERLY L. ANDERSON

Transgender. Bigender. Asexual. Panromantic. Kinkster. Pagan. Autistic. Polyamorous. Queer. Poet. Writer. More.

She/Her or They/Them

Beverly L. Anderson started writing at eleven, and when they did, it was apparent they would stick to something other than the every day. Her first story, written in spiral notebooks, was about a kidnapping. There were endless story ideas featuring fantastic places, monstrous creatures, and forbidden love in her mind even then. There's no surprise that these days, they favor the dark corners of the psyche over the happy and fluffy parts. Enamored with the mind, she studied extensively in psychology and related fields. She spends most of her days dreaming about stories and deciding how to make the unruly characters do as they tell them. As everyone knows, sometimes the characters take off and do what they want, no matter what the author has planned.

Beverly's other hobbies include gaming of all types, including a great love of tabletop, transgender and autism advocacy, and writing fanfiction when she can. Their interest in the BDSM community began as a simple curiosity but has led her to the road to finding a place for herself there as a Domme. She has gone on the journey of self-discovery in the last few years, finally pinning down their identity after nearly thirty years of searching. Coming out as bigender, asexual, panromantic, and polyamorous was one of the hardest things they've ever done, but it gave them the confidence to become themselves even more. An autistic person and an eclectic pagan, Beverly finds themself at odds with a lot of what society calls "normal." They don't mind, though, because they find that they are uniquely queer in every aspect of her life, and she's just fine with that.

Beverly started their writing journey seriously in 2013 when she found their way to fanfiction. She spent several years writing over three million words in various fandoms. In the last few years, they have been drawn to making those stories into original pieces and publishing them for a wider audience. Finding her publishing home helped make that dream a reality, one that they try to help others find.

Visit online: https://www.phoenixreal.net/

Also by Beverly L. Anderson

Crimson Hunt - Behind the Red Part One

Kerry Graham surprises his father by coming out as gay and cross-dresser and possibly non-binary. Then again, when he starts performing in drag at a local Cabaret named The Red, where his cousin works as a tailor. He finds himself free and able to be himself in a world that has always treated him as an outcast. He's among people that understand him, and he can finally relax. At least, that's what he believes. Then, a dress arrives, seemingly an apology for a bit of bigotry from a shop clerk. No one thinks a dress can cause any harm, so he wears it under the stage lights. Things go awry, though, and Kerry wonders what could possibly be happening. A bounty hunter named Martin swoops in, convinced that he can be of aid in the situation. Along with Martin, there's an intrepid FBI agent named Zak on the trail of a pair of sadistic serial killers who target and manipulate young, attractive, feminine men like Kerry.

Kerry doesn't believe it at first. Can he be targeted by these people? Then, things start happening, and his phone and email is full of messages with horrible images of what these people plan to do to him. He's frightened but staunch in living his life. He is adamant that he won't let them win, no matter what they do to him. Still, as the manipulation and gaslighting continue from afar, he starts to doubt everything he's ever known. He begins to lose purchase on reality but finds that Martin and Zak ground him. He refuses to give in to their sadistic games, but in the end, he begins to wonder if his willpower is enough to keep these people away from him.

***

Stolen Innocence - Doctor's Training Part One

When desperate criminals find an easy target in the autistic neurosurgeon Kieran Sung, the young doctor is soon at the mercy of a local Irish mob boss with perverse desires. Despite suffering at his hands, rescue finds him with relative quickness. Pulled unwillingly into circumstances that bring his world crashing down around him and destroying the carefully laid routines and structure he desires; Kieran must find a new way to live. He discovers comfort in ways he never imagined, within sensations of pressure and binding. Taking the hand of a childhood friend who desires nothing else but to help him, Kieran realizes his heart aches for more in his life. Circumstances bind him to a tattoo artist named Varick Jaeger, an actor named Carmine DeAngelo, and a bartender named Devan Sullivan. With this unlikely trio, Kieran must learn how to handle the upheaval in a life he sees desperately needs change.

Stolen Innocence, part one of the Doctor's Training Trilogy, is a story of healing that examines D/s culture, the complexities of polyamory, and how people often deal with mental and physical trauma. Follow Kieran, Devan, Varick, Carmine, and the rest of their pack; they navigate a world that rarely accepts people who do not fit in with expectations.

***

Dark and the Sword – Legacy of the Phoenix Book One

The world of Avern has moved on. It has been almost a thousand years since the day the entire pantheon disappeared. Since the Abandonment, the mortals have learned to live without gods and goddesses. The world became mundane, with little magic and even less hope. Tyrants have risen, and those able to wield what is left of magic are powerful. Forces surge in the darkness that threaten to topple the already fragile world. However, the plight of the world of Avern is not unknown, and those who watch from a distance have decided to intervene. The mortals are sleeping, however, unknowing that two great powers will soon be vying for control.

Then something happens that changes things. A young princess makes a bid for power by murdering her father. She then attempts to murder her sister, the crown princess of Lineria, Keiara. Despite a true strike aided by dark powers, Keiara doesn't die. Instead, the strike pierces the barrier between her human soul and the soul sleeping within her, the soul of the Dark Phoenix. More than a goddess, the Dark Phoenix is the legendary mother of the gods. She is a part of the Eternal Phoenix that brought life to their world eons ago, one of the primal forces of the cosmos.

***

Chasing the Silver Dragon – Part One Disconnect, Book One of the Dragon Trinity Cycle

Silver Dragon has become a bane to the werewolf community in recent years. Designer heroin, one that actually affects were creatures where normal drugs are simply a passing fancy, has infiltrated the St. Louis werewolves. One of these, a young woman named Anna Maddox, wants her brother back somehow from the brink he's standing at. To do this, she reaches out to the ancient order, the Children of Asclepius. Duncan Powell hears her plea and pledges to help her rescue her brother from the streets of St Louis.

He goes to Detective Sebastian Pearce, a member of Unit Zero, the law enforcement agency that deals with supernatural creatures that pose a threat to the peace in the world. Sebastian implores him to leave things to Unit Zero, but Duncan is stubborn and goes down to the Red District to find the young Were. Sebastian and his partner follow and then begin the mission that will either save Kacey Maddox or doom all of them.

***

Let Sparks Fly – Short Story Compilation

Romance can come from the most unexpected places. Sometimes, two people meet, and the sparks just fly between them. Then, sometimes, two people see each other every day, and don't realize the spark that exists between them.

In this volume, you will find stories of many kinds. You'll meet a pair of fellows just looking for a sub to share when they ask out two people, and a secret is revealed. A young man is pining for his very best (straight) friend when a strange entity shows him pleasures beyond imagining, along with some truth. Join a guy who secretly harbors a taboo wish he thinks will never come true. Watch the sparks as a pair of swimming rivals find themselves in a compromising position. A demon on a mountain demands a sacrifice and receives something he isn't expecting. And finally, a man finds his bliss in a woman who can completely own him.

Journey through these pages and enjoy short erotic stories of love found in some quite unusual ways.

***

Whispered Shadows – A Poetry Anthology

The twisting paths of a poet's mind lead to intriguing places, there can be little doubt of this. These places contain whispers of the writer's soul. Some paths show desired sights; others uncover unforeseen knowledge and, at times, unwanted things. The shadows conceal unknown discoveries on well-lit paths through the poet's mind. Travelers, beware: uncertain destinations await along these paths. Tread carefully. Becoming lost in the pages of the poet's thoughts may be a very real danger to these travelers.

So, come along and visit this place of shadows. Here, there be dragons, monsters, truth, and more to enjoy. Fantasy, Reality, and Truths form one hundred and fifty poems by Beverly L. Anderson. The first path is one of fantasy with mythic beasts of yore and darkness that creeps into the very bone. Fairies may fly, and dragons may soar. The second path is one of reality and perhaps questions of what is and is not within that reality. Questions of existence and what the world shows us daily are spoken here. And the final path is one of truths. These truths may be surprisingly uncomfortable or may not be the truth expected. In any case, travel the paths at your own risk.

Open these pages and see if something draws you into the whispered shadows of the very soul.

***

Reflections of the Shadow Dancer

In an abandoned dance studio, there's music and dancing unheard and unseen by anyone. The whispers in the shadows laud praises upon the figure who spins around the room, her body translucent and flickering in the night. Nothing is in motion, and yet everything moves around the room. Darkness and light intertwine and dance to cast the shadows of the world. The Shadow Dancer performs a dance that crosses the borders between the world and other surprising places within flickering shadows.

The Shadow Dancer knows the truth. Without the darkness, there can be no light. Without the light, there can be no darkness. Between them lies the shadow in which the Shadow Dancer twirls.

Enter the world of the Shadow Dancer and immerse yourself in 150 poems, living in the light, the dark, and the shadow.

Milton Keynes UK
Ingram Content Group UK Ltd.
UKHW010233111224
452348UK00011B/722